Jack Kerouac was born in 1922 in Lowell, Massachusetts, the youngest of three children in a French–Canadian family. In high school he was a star player on the local football team, and went on to win football scholarships to Horace Mann, a New York prep school, and Columbia College. He left Columbia and football in his sophomore year, joined the Merchant Marine and began the restless wanderings that were to continue for the greater part of his life.

His first novel, *The Town and the City*, was published in 1950. *On the Road*, although written in 1952 (in a few hectic days on a scroll of newsprint), was not published until 1957 – it made him one of the most controversial and best-known writers of his time. The publication of his many other books – among them *The Subterraneans, The Dharma Bums, Big Sur, Doctor Sax, Desolation Angels* – followed.

Kerouac died in 1969, in Orlando, Florida, at the age of forty-six.

'Vintage Kerouac . . . a helter-skelter diary . . . the record of a lost weekend, high on words'
Times Literary Supplement

KU-247-772

By the same author

JACK KEROUAC

Satori in Paris

GRANADA
London Toronto Sydney New York

Published by Granada Publishing Limited in 1982

ISBN 0 586 05545 2

First published in Great Britain by
Andre Deutsch Limited 1967
Copyright © Jack Kerouac 1966

Granada Publishing Limited
Frogmore, St Albans, Herts AL2 2NF
and
36 Golden Square, London W1R 4AH
515 Madison Avenue, New York, NY 10022, USA
117 York Street, Sydney, NSW 2000, Australia
100 Skyway Avenue, Rexdale, Ontario, M9W 3A6, Canada
61 Beach Road, Auckland, New Zealand

Printed and bound in Great Britain
by Cox and Wyman Ltd, Reading

Set in Times

This book is sold subject to the condition that it
shall not, by way of trade or otherwise, be lent,
re-sold, hired out or otherwise circulated
without the publisher's prior consent in any
form of binding or cover other than that in
which it is published and without a similar
condition including this condition being imposed
on the subsequent purchaser.

Granada ®
Granada Publishing ®

1

Somewhere during my ten days in Paris (and Brittany) I received an illumination of some kind that seems to've changed me again, towards what I suppose'll be my pattern for another seven years or more: in effect, a *satori*: the Japanese word for 'sudden illumination', 'sudden awakening', or simply 'kick in the eye.' – Whatever, something *did* happen and in my first reveries after the trip and I'm back home regrouping all the confused rich events of those ten days, it seems the satori was handed to me by a taxi driver named Raymond Baillet, other times I think it might've been my paranoiac fear in the foggy streets of Brest Brittany at 3 a.m., other times I think it was Monsieur Casteljaloux and his dazzlingly beautiful secretary (a Bretonne with blue-black hair, green eyes, separated front teeth just right in eatable lips, white wool knit sweater, with gold bracelets and perfume) or the waiter who told me *'Paris est pourri'* (Paris is rotten) or the performance of Mozart's Requiem in old church of St-Germain-des-Prés with elated violinists swinging their elbows with joy because so many distinguished people had shown up crowding the pews and special chairs (and outside it's misting) or, in Heaven's name, *what*? The straight tree lanes of Tuileries Gardens? Or the roaring sway of the bridge over the booming holiday Seine which I crossed holding on to my hat knowing it was not the bridge (the makeshift one at Quai des Tuileries) but I myself swaying from too much cognac and nerves and no sleep and jet airliner all the way from Florida twelve hours with airport anxieties, or bars, or anguishes, intervening?

As in an earlier autobiographical book I'll use my real name here, full name in this case, Jean-Louis Lebris de

Kérouac, because this story is about my search for this name in France, and I'm not afraid of giving the real name of Raymond Baillet to public scrutiny because all I have to say about him, in connection with the fact he may be the cause of my satori in Paris, is that he was polite, kind, efficient, hip, aloof and many other things and mainly just a cabdriver who happened to drive me to Orly airfield on my way back home from France: and sure he wont be in trouble because of that – And besides probably never will see his name in print because there are so many books being published these days in America and in France nobody has time to keep up with all of them, and if told by someone that his name appears in an American 'novel' he'll probably never find out where to buy it in Paris, if it's ever translated at all, and if he does find it, it wont hurt him to read that he, Raymond Baillet, is a great gentleman and cabdriver who happened to impress an American during a fare ride to the airport.

Compris?

2

But as I say I dont know how I got that Satori and the only
thing to do is start at the beginning and maybe I'll find out
right at the pivot of the story and go rejoicing to the end of it,
the tale that's told for no other reason but companionship,
which is another (and my favorite) definition of literature,
the tale that's told for companionship and to teach
something religious, or religious reverence, about real life, in
this real world which literature should (and here does)
reflect.

In other words, and after this I'll shut up, made-up stories
and romances about what would happen IF are for children
and adult cretins who are afraid to read themselves in a book
just as they might be afraid to look in the mirror when
they're sick or injured or hungover or *insane*.

3

This book'll say, in effect, have pity on us all, and dont get mad at me for writing at all.

I live in Florida. Arriving over Paris suburbs in the big Air France jetliner I noticed how green the northern countryside is in the summer, because of winter snows that have melted right into that butterslug meadow. Greener than any palmetto country could ever be, and especially in June before August (Août) has withered it all away. The plane touched down without a Georgia hitch. Here I'm referring to that planeload of prominent respectable Atlantans who were all loaded with gifts around 1962 and heading back to Atlanta when the liner shot itself into a farm and everybody died, it never left the ground and half of Atlanta was depleted and all the gifts were strewn and burned all over Orly, a great Christian tragedy not the fault of the French government at all since the pilots and steward's crew were all French citizens.

The plane touched down just right and here we were in Paris on a gray cold morning in June.

In the airport bus an American expatriate was calmly and joyfully smoking his pipe and talking to his buddy just arrived on another plane probably from Madrid or something. In my own plane I had not talked to the tired American painter girl because she fell asleep over Nova Scotia in the lonesome cold after the exhaustion of New York and having to buy a million drinks for the people who were babysitting there for her – no business of mine anyhow. She'd wondered at Idlewild if I was going to look up my old flame in Paris:– no. (I really shoulda.)

For I was the loneliest man in Paris if that's possible. It

was 6 A.M. and raining and I took the airport bus into the city, to near Les Invalides, then a taxi in the rain and I asked the driver where Napoleon was entombed because I knew it was someplace around there, not that it matters, but after a period of what I thought to be surly silence he finally pointed and said '*là*' (there).

I was all hot to go see the Sainte Chapelle where St Louis, King Louis IX of France, had installed a piece of the True Cross. I never even made it except ten days later zipping by in Raymond Baillet's cab and he mentioned it. I was also all hot to see St Louis de France church on the island of St Louis in the Seine River, because that's the name of the church of my baptism in Lowell, Massachusetts. Well I finally got there and sat with hat in hand watching guys in red coats blow long trumpets at the altar, to organ upstairs, beautiful Medieval *cansòs* or cantatas to make Handel's mouth water, and all of a sudden a woman with kids and husband comes by and lays twenty centimes (4¢) in my poor tortured misunderstood hat (which I was holding upsidedown in awe), to teach them *caritas*, or loving charity, which I accepted so's not to embarrass her teacherly instincts, or the kids, and my mother said back home in Florida 'Why didnt you then put the twenty centimes in the poor box' which I forgot. It wasnt enough to wonder about and besides the very first thing I did in Paris after I cleaned up in my hotel room (with a big round wall in it, welling the chimney I guess) was give a franc (20¢) to a French woman beggar with pimples, saying '*Un franc pour la Française*' (A franc for the Frenchwoman) and later I gave a franc to a man beggar in St-Germain to whom I then yelled: '*Vieux voyou!*' (Old hoodlum!) and he laughed and said: 'What? – *Hood*-lum?' I said 'Yes, you cant fool an old French Canadian' and I wonder today if that hurt him because what I really wanted to say was 'Guenigiou' (ragpicker) but 'voyou' came out.

Guenigiou it is.

(Ragpicker should be spelled 'guenillou', but that's not the

9

way it comes out in 300-year-old French which was preserved intact in Quebec and still understood in the streets of Paris not to mention the hay barns of the North.)

Coming down the steps of that magnificent huge church of La Madeleine was a dignified old bum in a full brown robe and gray beard, neither a Greek nor a Patriarch, just probably an old member of the Syriac Church; either that or a Surrealist on a larky kick? Na.

4

First things first.

The altar in La Madeleine is a gigantic marble sculpt of her (Mary Magdalena) as big as a city block and surrounded by angels and archangels. She holds out her hands in a gesture Michelangeloesque. The angels have huge wings dripping. The place is a whole city block long. It's a long narrow building of a church, one of the strangest. No spires, no Gothic, but I suppose Greek temple style. (Why on earth would you, or did you, expect me to go see the Eiffel Tower made of Bucky Buckmaster's steel ribs and ozone? How dull can you get riding an elevator and getting the mumps from being a quarter mile in the air? I already done that orf the Hempire State Building at night in the mist with my editor.)

The taxi took me to the hotel which was a Swiss pension I guess but the nightclerk was an Etruscan (same thing) and the maid was sore at me because I kept my door and suitcase locked. The lady who ran the hotel was not pleased when I inaugurated my first evening with a wild sexball with a woman my age (43). I cant give her real name but it's one of the oldest names in French history, aye back before Charlemagne, and he was a Pippin. (Prince of the Franks.) (Descended from Arnulf, L'Évêque of Metz). (Imagine having to fight Frisians, Alemanni, Bavarians *and* Moors.) (Grandson of Plectrude.) Well this old gal was the wildest lay imaginable. How can I go into such detail about toilet matters. She really made me blush at one point. I shoulda told her to stick her head in the 'poizette' but of course (that's Old French for toilette) she was too delightful for words. I met her in an afterhours Montparnasse gangster bar with no gangsters around. She took me over. She also wants

11

to marry me, naturally, as I am a great natural bed mate and nice guy. I gave her $120 for her son's education, or some new–old parochial shoes. She really done my budget in. I still had enough money the next day to go on and buy William Makepeace Thackeray's *Livres des Snobs* at Gare St-Lazare. It isnt a question of money but souls having a good time. In the old church of St-Germain-des-Prés that following afternoon I saw several Parisian Frenchwomen practically weeping as they prayed under an old bloodstained and rainroiled wall. I said 'Ah ha, *les femmes de Paris*' and I saw the greatness of Paris that it can weep for the follies of the Revolution and at the same time rejoice they got rid of all those long nosed nobles, of which I am a descendant (Princes of Brittany).

5

Chateaubriand was an amazing writer who wanted early old love affairs on a higher order than the Order was giving him in 1790 France – he wanted something out of a Medieval vignette, some young gal come down the street and look him right in the eye, with ribbons and a grandmother sewing, and that night the house burns down. Me and my Pippin had our healthy get-together at some point or other in my very calm drunkenness and I was satisfied, but next day I didnt wanta see her no mo because she wanted *more* money. Said she was going to take me out on the town. I told her she owed me several more jobs, bouts, jots and tittles.

'*Mais oui.*'

But I let the Etruscan fluff her off on the phone.

The Etruscan was a pederast. In which I have no interest, but $120 is going too far. The Etruscan said he was a Mountain Italian. I dont care or know if he's a pederast or not, actually, and shouldna said that, but he was a nice kid. I then went out and got drunk. I was about to meet some of the prettiest women in the world but the bed business was over because now I was getting real stoned drunk.

6

It's hard to decide what to tell in a story, and I always seem to try to prove something, comma, about my sex. Let's forget it. It's just that sometimes I get terribly lonely, for the companionship of a woman dingblast it.

So I spend all day in St-Germain looking for the perfect bar and I find it. *La Gentilhommière* (Rue St André des Arts, which is pointed out to me by a gendarme) – Bar of the Gentle Lady – And how gentle can you get with soft blonde hair all golden sprayed and neat little figure? 'O I wish I was handsome' I say but they all assure me I'm handsome – 'Alright then I'm a dirty old drunk' – 'Anything you want to say'—

I gaze into her eyes – I give her the double whammy blue eyes compassion shot – She falls for it.

A teenage Arab girl from Algiers or Tunis comes in, with a soft little hook nose. I'm going out of my mind because meanwhile I'm exchanging a hundred thousand French pleasantries and conversations with Negro Princes from Senegal, Breton Surrealist poets, boulevardiers in perfect clothes, lecherous gynecologists (from Brittany), a Greek bartender angel called Zorba, and the owner is Jean Tassart cool and calm by his cash register and looking vaguely depraved (tho actually a quiet family man who happens to look like Rudy Loval my old buddy in Lowell Massachusetts who'd had such a reputation at fourteen for his many *amours* and had that same perfume of smoothy looks). Not to mention Daniel Maratra the other bartender, some weird tall Jew or Arab, in any case a Semite, whose name sounded like the trumpets in front of the walls of Granada: and a gentler tender of bar you never saw.

In the bar there's a woman who is a lovely 40-year-old redhead Spaniard *amoureuse* who takes an actual liking to me, does worse and takes me seriously, and actually makes a date for us to meet alone: I get drunk and forget. Over the speaker is coming endless American modern jazz over a tape. To make up for forgetting to meet Valarino (the redhead Spanish beauty) I buy her a tapestry on the Quai, from a young Dutch genius, ten bucks (Dutch genius whose name in Dutch, Beere, means 'pier' in English). She announces she's going to redecorate her room on account of it but doesnt invite me over. What I woulda done to her shall be not allowed in this Bible yet it woulda been spelled LOVE.

I get so mad I go down to the whore districts. A million Apaches with daggers are milling around. I go in a hallway and I see three ladies of the night. I announce with an evil English leer '*Sh'prend la belle brunette*' (I take the pretty brunette) – The brunette rubs her eyes, throat, ears and heart and says 'I aint gonna have that no more.' I stomp away and take out my Swiss Army knife with the cross on it, because I suspect I'm being followed by French muggers and thugs. I cut my own finger and bleed all over the place. I go back to my hotel room bleeding all over the lobby. The Swiss woman by now is asking me when I'm going to leave. I say 'I'll leave as soon as I've verified my family in the library.' (And add to myself: 'What do you know about *les Lebris de Kérouacks* and their motto of Love Suffer and Work you dumb old Bourgeois bag.')

7

So I go to the library, la Bibliothèque Nationale, to check up
on the list of the officers in Montcalm's Army 1756 Quebec,
and also Louis Moréri's dictionary, and Père Anselme etc.,
all the information about the royal house of Brittany, and it
aint even there and finally in the Mazarine Library old sweet
Madame Oury the head librarian patiently explains to me
that the Nazis done bombed and burned all their French
papers in 1944, something which I'd forgotten in my zeal.
Still I smell that there's something fishy in Brittany – Surely
de Kérouack should be recorded in France if it's already
recorded in the British Museum in London? – I tell her
that—

You cant smoke even in the toilet in the Bibliothèque
Nationale and you cant get a word in edgewise with the
secretaries and there's a national pride about 'scholars' all
sitting there copying outa books and they wouldnt even let
John Montgomery in (John Montgomery who forgot his
sleeping bag on the climb to Matterhorn and is America's
best librarian and scholar and is English)—

Meanwhile I have to go back and see how the gentle ladies
are doing. My cabdriver is Roland Ste Jeanne d'Arc de la
Pucelle who tells me that all Bretons are 'corpulent' like me.
The ladies are kissing me on both cheeks French style. A
Breton called Goulet is getting drunk with me, young, 21,
blue eyes, black hair, and suddenly grabs Blondie and scares
her (with the other fellows joining in), almost a rape, which
me and the other Jean, Tassart, put a stop to: 'Awright!'
'Arrête!'—

'Cool it,' I add.

She is just too beautiful for words. I said to her 'Tu passe *toutes la journée dans maudite* beauty parlor?' (You spend all day in the damn beauty parlor?)

'*Oui.*'

Meanwhile I go down to the famous cafes on the boulevard and sit there watching Paris go by, such hepcats the young men, motorcycles, visiting firemen from Iowa.

8

The Arab girl goes out with me, I invite her to see and hear a performance of Mozart's Requiem in old St-Germain-des-Prés church, which I knew about from an earlier visit and saw the poster announcing it. It's full of people, crowded, we pay at the door and walk into surely the most *distingué* gathering in Paris that night, and as I say it's misting outside, and her soft little hook nose has under it rose lips.

I teach her Christianity.

We neck a little later and she goes home to her parents. She wants me to take her to the beach at Tunis, I'm wondering if I shall be stabbed by Arabs jealous on the Bikini beach and that week Boumedienne deposed and *dis*posed of Ben Bella and that woulda been a fine kettle of fish, and also I didnt have the money now and I wonder why she wanted that:– I've been told where to get off on the beaches of Morocco.

I just dont know.

Methinks women love me and then they realize I'm drunk for all the world and this makes them realize I cant concentrate on them alone, for long, makes them jealous, and I'm a fool in Love With God. Yes.

Besides, lechery's not my meat and makes me blush:– depends on the Lady. She was not my style. The French blonde was, but too young for me.

In times to come I'll be known as the fool who rode outa Mongolia on a pony: Genghiz Khan, or the Mongolian Idiot, *one*. Well I'm not an idiot, and I like ladies, and I'm polite, but impolitic, like Ippolit my cousin from Russia. An old hitch hiker in San Francisco, called Joe Ihnat, announced that mine was an ancient Russian name meaning

'Love'. Kerouac. I said 'Then they went to Scotland?'

'Yes, then Ireland, then Cornwall, Wales, and Brittany, then you know the rest.'

'*Roos*hian?'

'Means Love.'

'You're kidding.'

—Oh, and then I realized, 'of course, outa Mongolia and the Khans, and before that, Eskimos of Canada and Siberia. All goes back around the world, not to mention Perish-the-Thought Persia.' (Aryans).

Anyhow me and the Breton Goulet went to an evil bar where a hundred assorted Parisians were eagerly listening to a big argument between a white man and a black man. I got outa there quick and left him to his own devices, met him back at La Gentilhommière, some fight musta spilled out, or, not, I wasnt there.

Paris is a tough town.

9

The fact of the matter is, how can you be an Aryan when you're an Eskimo or a Mongol? That old Joe Ihnat was full of little brown turds, unless he means Russia. Old Joe Tolstoy we shoulda picked up.

Why keep talking about such things? Because my grammar school teacher was Miss Dineen, who is now Sister Mary of St James in New Mexico (James was a son of Mary, like Jude), and she wrote: 'Jack and his sister Carolyn (Ti Nin) I remember well as friendly, co-operative children with unusual charm. We were told that their folks came from France, and that the name was de Kerouac. I always felt that they had the dignity and refinement of aristocracy.'

I mention this to show that there can be such a thing as manners.

My manners, abominable at times, can be sweet. As I grew older I became a drunk. Why? Because I like ecstasy of the mind.

I'm a Wretch.

But I love love.

(Strange Chapter)
10

Not only that but you cant get a night's sleep in France, they're so lousy and noisy at 8 A.M. screaming over fresh bread it would make Abomination weep. Buy that. Their strong hot coffee and *croissants* and crackling French bread and Breton butter, Gad, where's my Alsatian beer?

While looking for the library, incidentally, a gendarme in the Place de la Concorde told me that Rue de Richelieu (street of the National Library) was thataway, pointing, and because he was an officer I was afraid to say '*What? . . .*NO!' because I knew it was in the opposite direction somewhere – Here he is some kind of sergeant or other who certainly oughta know the streets of Paris giving an American tourist a bum steer. (Or did he believe I was a wise-guy Frenchman pulling his leg? since my French *is* French) – But no, he points in the direction of one of de Gaulle's security buildings and sends me there maybe thinking 'That's the National Library alright, ha ha ha' ('maybe they'll shoot down that Quebec rat') – Who knows? Any Parisian middle-aged gendarme oughta know where Rue de Richelieu is – But thinking he may be right and I'd made a mistake studying the Paris map back home I do go in the direction he points, afraid to go any other, and go down the upper spate of Champs-Elysées then cut across the damp green park and across Rue Gabriel to the back of an important government building of some kind where suddenly I see a sentry box and out of it steps a guard with bayonet in full Republican Guard regalia (like Napoleon with a cockatoo hat) and he snaps to attention and holds up his bayonet at *Present Arms* but it's not for me really, it's for a sudden black limousine full of bodyguards and guys in black suits who receive a salute from the other sentry men and zip on by – I stroll past the sentry bayonet and take out my plastic Camel cigarette container to light a butt – Immediately two strolling gendarmes are passing me in the opposite direction watching every move I make – It turns out I'm only lighting a butt but how can they tell? *plastic* and all that – And that is the marvelous tight security around big old de Gaulle's very palace which is a few blocks away.

I go down to the corner bar to have a cognac alone at a cool table by the open door.

The bartender there is very polite and tells me exactly how to get to the library: right down St-Honoré then across la Place de la Concorde and then Rue Rivoli right at the Louvre and left on Richelieu to the Library dingblast it.

So how can an American tourist who doesnt speak French get around at all? Let alone me?

To know the name of the street of the sentry box itself I'd have to order a map from the CIA.

11

A strange severe parochial-style library, la Bibliothèque Nationale on rue de Richelieu, with thousands of scholars and millions of books and strange assistant librarians with Zen Master brooms (really French aprons) who admire good *handwriting* more than anything in a scholar or writer – Here, you feel like an American genius who escaped the rules of Le Lycée. (French High School).

All I wanted was: *Histoire généalogique de plusieurs maisons illustres de Bretagne, enrichie des arms et blasons d'icelles . . .* etc. by Fr Augustin Du Paz, Paris, N.Buon, 1620, Folio Lm² 23 et Rés. Lm 23.

Think I got it? Not on your—

And also I wanted:– Père Anselme de Sainte Marie. (*né* Pierre de Guibours), his *Histoire de la maison royale de France, des puirs, grands officiers de la couronne et de la maison du roy et des anciens barons du royaume*, R. P. Anselme, Paris, E. Loyson 1674, Lm³ 397, (History of the royal house of France, and of also, the great officers of the crown and of the house of the king and of the ancient barons of the kingdom), all of which I had to write down neatly as I could on the call-cards and the old aproned fella told the old lady librarian 'It's well written' (meaning the legibility of the handwriting). Of course they all smelled the liquor on me and thought I was a nut but on seeing I knew what and how to ask for certain books they all went in back to huge dusty files and shelves as high as the roof and must've drawn up ladders high enough to make Finnegan fall again with an even bigger noise than the one in Finnegans Wake, this one being the noise of the name, the actual name the Indian Buddhists gave to the Tathagata or passer-through of the

23

Aeon Priyadavsana more than Incalculable Aeons ago:–
Here we go, Finn:–

GALADHARAGARGITAGHOSHASUSVARA-
NAKSHATRARAGASANKUSUMITABHIGNA.

Now I mention this to show, that if I didnt know libraries,
and specifically the greatest library in the world, the New
York Public Library where I among a thousand other things
actually copied down this long Sanskrit name exactly as it's
spelled, then why should I be regarded with suspicion in the
Paris Library? Of course I'm not young any more and 'smell
of liquor' and even talk to interesting Jewish scholars in the
library there (one Éli Flamand copying down notes for a
history of Renaissance art and who kindly assisted me's
much's he could), still I dont know, it seemed they really
thought I was nuts when they saw what I asked for, which I
copied from their *incorrect* and incomplete files, not fully
what I showed you above about Père Anselme as written in
the completely correct files of London, as I found later where
the national records were not destroyed by fire, saw what I
asked for, which did not conform to the actual titles of the
old books they had in the back, and when they saw my name
Kerouac but with a 'Jack' in front of it, as tho I were a
Johann Maria Philipp Frimont von Palota suddenly
traveling from Staten Island to the Vienna Library and
signing my name on the call-cards as Johnny Pelota and
asking for Hergott's *Genealogia augustae gentis Habsburgicae*
(incomplete title) and my name not spelled 'Palota', as it
should, just as my real name should be spelled 'Kerouack',
but both old Johnny and me've been thru so many centuries
of genealogical wars and crests and cockatoos and gules and
jousts against Fitzwilliams, agh—
    It doesnt matter.
    And besides it's all too long ago and worthless unless you
can find the actual family monuments in fields, like with me I

go claim the bloody dolmens of Carnac? Or I go and claim the Cornish language which is called Kernuak? Or some little old cliff–castle at Kenedjack in Cornwall or one of the 'hundreds' called Kerrier in Cornwall? Or Cornouialles itself outside Quimper and Keroual? (Brittany thar).

Well anyway I was trying to find things out about my old family, I was the first Lebris de Kérouack ever to go back to France in 210 years to find out and I was planning to go to Brittany and Cornwall England next (land of Tristan and King Mark) and later I was gonna hit Ireland and find Isolde and like Peter Sellers get banged in the mug in a Dublin pub.

Ridiculous, but I was so happy on cognac I was going to try.

The whole library groaned with the accumulated debris of centuries of recorded folly, as tho you had to record folly in the Old or the New World anyhow, like my closet with its incredible debris of cluttered old letters by the thousands, books, dust, magazines, childhood boxscores, the likes of which when I woke up the other night from a pure sleep, made me groan to think this is what I was doing with my waking hours: burdening myself with junk neither I nor anybody else should really want or will ever remember in Heaven.

Anyway, an example of my troubles at the library. They didnt bring me those books. On opening them I think they would have cracked apart. What I really shoulda done is say to that head librarian:– 'I'm gonna put you in a horseshoe and give you to a horse to wear in the Battle of Chickamauga.'

12

Meanwhile I kept asking everybody in Paris 'Where's Pascal buried? Where's Balzac's cemetery?' Somebody finally told me Pascal must certainly be buried out of town at Port Royal near his pious sister, Jansenists, and as for Balzac's cemetery I didnt wanta go to no cemetery at midnight (Père Lachaise) and anyway as we were blasting along in a wild taxi ride at 3 a.m. near Montparnasse they yelled 'There's your Balzac! His statue on the square!'

'Stop the cab!' and I got out, swept off me hat in sweeping bow, saw the statue vaguely gray in the drunken misting streets, and that was that. And how could I find my way to Port Royal if I could hardly find my way back to my hotel?

And besides they're not there at all, only their bodies.

13

Paris is a place where you can really walk around at night and find what you dont want, O Pascal.

Trying to make my way to the Opera a hundred cars came charging around a blind curve–corner and like all the other pedestrians I waited to let them pass and then they all started across but I waited a few seconds looking the other charging cars over, all coming from six directions – Then I stepped off the curb and a car came around that curve all alone like the chaser running last in a Monaco race and right at me – I stepped back just in time – At the wheel a Frenchman completely convinced that no one else has a right to live or get to his mistress as fast as he does – As a New Yorker I run to dodge the free zipping roaring traffic of Paris but Parisians just stand and then stroll and leave it to the driver – And by God it works, I saw dozens of cars screech to a stop from 70 m.p.h. to let some stroller have his way!

I was going to the Opera also to eat in any restaurant that looked nice, it was one of my sober evenings dedicated to solitary studious walks, but O what grim rainy Gothic buildings and me walking well in the middle of those wide sidewalks so's to avoid dark doorways – What vistas of Nowhere City Night and hats and umbrellas – I couldn't even buy a newspaper – Thousands of people were coming out of some performance somewhere – I went to a crowded restaurant on Boulevard des Italiens and sat way at the end of the bar by myself on a high stool and watched, wet and helpless, as waiters mashed up raw hamburg with Worcestershire sauce and other things and other waiters rushed by holding up steaming trays of good food – The one sympathetic counterman brought menu and Alsatian beer I ordered and I told him to wait awhile – He didnt understand that, drinking without eating at once, because he is partner to the secret of charming French eaters:– they rush at the very beginning with *hors d'oeuvres* and bread, and then plunge into their entrees (this is practically always before even a slug of wine) and then they slow down and start lingering, now the wine to wash the mouth, now comes the *talk*, and now the second half of the meal, wine, dessert and coffee, something I cannae do.

In any case I'm drinking my second beer and reading the menu and notice an American guy is sitting five stools away but he is so mean looking in his absolute disgust with Paris I'm afraid to say 'Hey, you American?' – He's come to Paris expecting he woulda wound up under a cherry tree in blossom in the sun with pretty girls on his lap and people dancing around him, instead he's been wandering the rainy streets alone in all that jargon, doesnt even know where the whore district is, or Notre Dame, or some small cafe they told him about back in Glennon's bar on Third Avenue, *nothing* – When he pays for his sandwich he literally throws the money on the counter 'You wouldnt help me figure what the real price is anyway, and besides shove it up your you-know-what I'm going back to my old mine nets in Norfolk and get drunk with Bill Eversole in the bookie joint and all the other things you dumb frogs dont know about,' and stalks out in poor misunderstood raincoat and disillusioned rubbers—

Then in come two American schoolteachers of Iowa, sisters on a big trip to Paris, they've apparently got a hotel room round the corner and aint left it except to ride the sightseeing buses which pick em up at the door, but they know this nearest restaurant and have just come down to buy a couple of oranges for tomorrow morning because the only oranges in France are apparently Valencias imported from Spain and too expensive for anything so avid as quick simple *break* of *fast*. So to my amazement I hear the first clear bell tones of American speech in a week:– 'You got some oranges here?'

'*Pardon?*' – the counterman.

'There they are in that glass case,' says the other gal.

'Okay – see?' pointing, 'two oranges,' and showing two fingers, and the counterman takes out the two oranges and puts em in a bag and says crisply thru his throat with those Arabic Parisian 'r's':–

'*Trois francs cinquante.*' In other words, 35¢ an orange but the old gals dont care what it costs and besides they dont understand what he's said.

'What's *that* mean?'

'*Pardon?*'

'Alright, I'll hold out my palm and take your kwok-kowk-kwark out of it, all we want's the oranges' and the two ladies burst into peals of screaming laughter like on the porch and the cat politely removes three francs fifty centimes from her hand, leaving the change, and they walk out lucky they're not alone like that American guy—

I ask my counterman what's real good and he says Alsatian Choucroute which he brings – It's just hotdogs, potatos and sauerkraut, but such hotdogs as chew like butter and have a flavor delicate as the scent of wine, butter and garlic all cooking together and floating out a cafe kitchen door – The sauerkraut no better'n Pennsylvania, potatos we got from Maine to San Jose, but O yes I forgot:– with it all, on top, is a weird soft strip of bacon which is really like ham and is the best bite of all.

I had come to France to do nothing but walk and eat and this was my first meal and my last, ten days.

But in referring back to what I said to Pascal, as I was leaving this restaurant (paid 24 francs or almost $5 for this simple platter) I heard a howling in the rainy boulevard – A maniacal Algerian had gone mad and was shouting at everyone and everything and was holding something I couldnt see, very small knife or object or pointed ring or

29

something – I had to stop in the door – People hurried by scared – I didn't want to be *seen* by him hurrying away – The waiters came out and watched with me – He approached us stabbing outdoor wicker chairs as he came – The headwaiter and I looked calmy into each other's eyes as tho to say 'Are we together?' – But my counterman began talking to the mad Arab, who was actually light haired and probably half French half Algerian, and it became some sort of conversation and I walked around and went home in a now-driving rain, had to hail a cab.

Romantic raincoats.

14

In my room I looked at my suitcase so cleverly packed for
this big trip the idea of which began all the previous winter in
Florida reading Voltaire, Chateaubriand, de Montherlant
(whose latest book was even now displayed in the shop-
windows of Paris, 'The Man Who Travels Alone is a Devil')
– Studying maps, planning to walk all over, eat, find my
ancestors' home town in the Library and then go to Brittany
where it was and where the sea undoubtedly washed the
rocks – My plan being, after five days in Paris, go to that inn
on the sea in Finistère and go out at midnight in raincoat,
rain hat, with notebook and pencil and with large plastic bag
to write inside of, i.e., stick hand, pencil and notebook into
bag, and write dry, while rain falls on rest of me, write the
sounds of the sea, part two of poem 'Sea' to be entitled:
'SEA, Part Two, the Sounds of the Atlantic at X, Brittany,'
either at outside of Carnac, or Concarneau, or Pointe de
Penmarch, or Douarnenez, or Plouzaimedeau, or Brest, or
St Malo – There in my suitcase, the plastic bag, the two
pencils, the extra leads, the notebook, the scarf, the sweater,
the raincoat in the closet, and the warm shoes—

   The warm shoes indeed, I'd also brought from Florida air-
conditioned shoes anticipating long hotsun walks in Paris
and hadnt worn them once, the 'warm shoes' were all I wore
the whole blessed time – In the Paris papers people were
complaining about the solid month of rain and cold
throughout late-May and early-June France as being caused
by scientists tampering with the weather.

   And my first aid kit, and my mittens for the cold midnight
musings on the Breton shore when the writing's done, and all
fancy sports shirts and extra socks I never even got to wear in

Paris let alone London where I'd also planned to go, not to mention Amsterdam and Cologne afterwards.

I was already homesick,

Yet this book is to prove that no matter how you travel, how 'successful' your tour, or foreshortened, you always learn something and learn to change your thoughts.

As usual I was simply concentrating everything in one intense but thousandéd 'Ah-*ha*!'

15

For instance the next afternoon after a good sleep, and me spruced up clean again, I met a Jewish composer or something from New York, with his bride, and somehow they liked me and anyway they were lonely and we had dinner, the which I didnt touch much as I hit up on cognac neat again – 'Let's go around the corner and see a movie,' he says, which we do after I've talked a half dozen eager French conversations around the restaurant with Parisians, and the movie turns out to be the last few scenes of O'Toole and Burton in 'Becket', very good, especially their meeting on the beach on horseback, and we say goodbye—

Again, I go into a restaurant right across from La Gentilhommière recommended to me highly by Jean Tassart, swearing this time I'll have a full course Paris dinner – I see a quiet man spooning a sumptuous soup in a huge bowl across the way and order it by saying 'The same soup as Monsieur.' It turns out to be a fish and cheese and red pepper soup as hot as Mexican peppers, terrific and *pink* – With this I have the fresh French bread and gobs of creamery butter but by the time they're ready to bring me the entree chicken roasted and basted with champagne and then sautéed in champagne, and the mashed salmon on the side, the anchovie, the Gruyère, and the little sliced cucumbers and the little tomatos red as cherries and then by God actual fresh cherries for dessert, all *mit* wine of vine, I have to apologize I cant even think of eating anything after all that (my stomach's shrunk by now, lost 15 pounds) – But the quiet soup gentleman moves on to a broiled fish and we actually start chatting across the restaurant and turns out he's the art dealer who sells Arps and Ernsts around the corner, knows André Breton, and wants me to visit his shop tomorrow. A marvelous man, and Jewish, and we have our conversation in French, and I even tell him that I roll my 'r's' on my tongue and not in my throat because I come from Medieval French Quebec-via-Brittany stock, and he agrees, admitting that modern Parisian French, tho dandy, *has* really been changed by the influx of Germans, Jews and Arabs for all these two centuries and not to mention the influence of the fops in the court of Louis Fourteenth which really started it all, and I also remind him that François Villon's real name was pronounced 'Ville On' and not 'Viyon' (which is a corruption) and that in those days you said not 'toi' or 'moi' but like 'twé' or 'mwé' (as we still do in Quebec and in two days I heard it in Brittany) but I finally warned him, concluding my charming lecture across the restaurant as people listened half amused and half attentive, François' name *was* pronounced François and not Françwé for the simple reason that he spelled it Françoy, like the King is spelled Roy, and this has nothing to do with 'oi' and if the King had ever heard it pronounced rouwé (rwé) he would not have invited you to the Versailles dance but given you a *roué* with a hood over his head to deal with your impertinent *cou*, or coup, and couped it right off and recouped you nothing but loss.

Things like that—

Maybe that's when my Satori took place. Or how. The amazing long sincere conversations in French with hundreds of people everywhere, was what I really liked, and did, and it was an accomplishment because they couldnt have replied in detail to my detailed points if they hadnt understood every word I said. Finally I began being so cocky I didn't even bother with Parisian French and let loose blasts and *pataraffes* of *charivarie* French that had them in stitches because they still understood, so there, Professor Sheffer and Professor Cannon (my old French 'teachers' in college and prep school who used to laugh at my 'accent' but gave me A's.)

But enough of that.

Suffice it to say, when I got back to New York I had more fun talking in Brooklyn accents'n I ever had in me life and especially when I got back down South, whoosh, what a miracle are different languages and what an amazing Tower of Babel this world is. Like, imagine going to Moscow or Tokyo or Prague and listening to all *that*.

That people actually understand what their tongues are babbling. And that eyes do shine to understand, and that responses are made which indicate a soul in all this matter and mess of tongues and teeth, mouths, cities of stone, rain, heat, cold, the whole wooden mess all the way from Neanderthaler grunts to Martian-probe moans of intelligent scientists, nay, all the way from the Johnny Hart ZANG of anteater tongues to the dolorous *'la notte, ch'i' passai con tanta pieta'* of Signore Dante in his understood shroud of robe ascending finally to Heaven in the arms of Beatrice.

Speaking of which I went back to see the gorgeous young blonde in La Gentilhommière and she piteously calls me 'Jacques' and I have to explain to her my name is 'Jean' and so she sobs her 'Jean', grins, and leaves with a handsome young boy and I'm left there hanging on the bar stool pestering everybody with my poor loneliness which goes unnoticed in the crashing busy night, in the smash of the cash register, the racket of washing glasses. I want to tell them that we dont all want to become ants contributing to the social body, but individualists each one counting one by one, but no, try to tell that to the in-and-outers rushing in and out the humming world night as the world turns on one axis. The secret storm has become a public tempest.

But Jean-Pierre Lemaire the Young Breton poet is tending the bar, sad and handsome as none but French youths can be, and very sympathetic with my silly position as a visiting drunkard alone in Paris, shows me a good poem about a hotel room in Brittany by the sea but after that shows me a meaningless surrealist-type poem about chicken bones on some girl's tongue ('Take it back to Cocteau!' I feel like yelling in English) but I don't want to hurt him, and he's been nice but's afraid to talk to me because he's on duty and crowds of people are at the outdoor tables waiting for their drinks, young lovers head to head, I'da done better staying home and painting the 'Mystical Marriage of St Catherine' after Girolamo Romanino but I'm so enslaved to yak and tongue, paint bores me, and it takes a lifetime to learn how to paint.

16

I meet Monsieur Casteljaloux in a bar across the street from church of St Louis de France and tell him about the library – He invites me to the National Archives the next day and will see what he can do – Guys are playing billiards in the back room and I'm watching real close because lately down South I've begun to shoot some real good pool especially when I'm drunk, which is another good reason to give up drinking, but they pay absolutely no attention to me as I keep saying '*Bon*!' (like an Englishman with handlebar mustache and no front teeth yelling 'Good Shot!' in a clubroom) – Billiards with no pockets however not my meat – I like pockets, holes, I like straightahead bank shots that are utterly impossible except with high inside-or-outside English, just a slice, hard, the ball clocks in and the cueball leaps up, one time it leaped up, rolled around the edges of the table and bounced back on the green and the game was over, as it was the eight-ball slotted in – (A shot referred to by my Southern pool partner Cliff Anderson as a 'Jesus Christ shot') – Naturally, being in Paris I wanta play some pool with the local talent and test Wits Transatlantique but they're not interested – As I say, I go to the National Archives on a curious street called Rue des Francs-Bourgeois (you might say, 'street of the outspoken middleclass,') surely a street you once saw old Balzac's floppy coat go flapping down on an urgent afternoon to his printer's galleys, or like the cobblestoned streets of Vienna when once Mozart did walk with floppy pants one afternoon on the way to his librettist, coughing)—

I'm directed into the main office of the Archives where Mr Casteljaloux wears today a melancholier look than the one he wore yesterday on his clean handsome ruddy blue eyed middleaged face – It tugs at my heart to hear him say that since he saw me yesterday, his mother's fallen seriously ill and he has to go to her now, his secretary will take care of everything.

She is, as I say, that ravishingly beautiful, unforgettably raunchily edible Breton girl with sea-green eyes, blueblack hair, little teeth with the slight front separation that, had she met a dentist who proposed to straighten them out, every man in the world shoulda strapped him to the neck of the wooden horse of Troy to let him have one look at captive Helen 'ere Paris beleaguered his treacherous and lecherous Gaulois Gullet.

Wearing a white knit sweater, golden bracelets and things, and perceiving me with her sea eyes, I ayed and almost saluted but only admitted to myself that such a woman were wronks and wars and not for me the peaceful shepherd mit de cognac – I'd a Eunuch been, to play with such proclivities and declivities two weeks—

I suddenly longed to go to England as she began to rattle off that there were only *manuscripts* in the National Archives and a lot of them had been burned in the Nazi bombing and besides they had no records there of '*les affaires Colonielles*' (Colonial matters).

'Colon*ielles*!' I yelled in a real rage glaring at her.

'Dont you have a list of the officers in Montcalm's Army in 1756?' I went on, getting to the point at least, but so mad at her for her Irish haughtiness (yes *Irish*, because all Bretons came from Ireland one way or the other before Gaul was called Gaul and Caesar saw a Druid tree stump and before Saxons showed up and before and after Pictish Scotland and so on), but no, she gives me that seagreen look and Ah, now I see her—

'My ancestor was an officer of the Crown, his name I just told you, and the year, he came from Brittany, he was a Baron they tell me, I'm the first of the family to return to France to look for the records.' But then I realized I was being haughtier, nay, not haughtier than she was but simpler than a street beggar to even talk like that or even try to find any records, making true or false, since as a Breton she probably knew it could only be found in Brittany as there had been a little war called *La Vendée* between Catholic Brittany and Republican Atheist Paris too horrible to mention a stone's throw from Napoleon's tomb—

The main fact was, she'd heard M Casteljaloux tell her all about me, my name, my quest, and it struck her as a silly thing to do, tho noble, noble in the sense of hopeless noble *try*, because Johnny Magee around the corner as anybody knows can, with any luck, find in Ireland that he's the descendant of the Morholt's King and so what? Johnny Anderson, Johnny Goldstein, Johnny Anybody, Lin Chin, Ti Pak, Ron Poodlewhorferer, Anybody.

And for me, an American, to handle manuscripts there, if any relating to my problem, what difference did it make?

I dont remember how I got out of there but the lady was not pleased and neither was I – But what I didnt know about Brittany at the time was that Quimper, in spite of its being the ancient capital of Cornouialles and the residence of its kings or hereditary counts and latterly the capital of the department of Finistère and all that, was nevertheless of all dumb bigcity things considered a hickplace by the popular wits of Paris, because of its distance from the capital, so that as you might say to a New York Negro 'If you dont do right I'm gonna send you back to Arkansas,' Voltaire and Condorcet would laugh and say 'If you dont understand aright we'll send you out to Quimper ha ha ha.' – Connecting that with Quebec and the famous dumb Canucks she musta laughed in her teeth.

I went, on somebody's tip, to the Bibliothèque Mazarine near Quai St Michel and nothing happened there either except the old lady librarian winked at me, gave me her name (Madame Oury), and told me to write to her anytime.

All there was to do in Paris was done.

I bought an air ticket to Brest, Brittany.

Went down to the bar to say goodbye to everybody and one of them, Goulet the Breton said, 'Be careful, they'll *keep* you there!'

P.S. As one last straw, before buying the ticket, I went over to my French publishers and announced my name and asked for the boss – The girl either believed that I was one of the authors of the house, which I am to the tune of six novels now, or not, but she coldly said that he was out to lunch—

'Alright then, where's Michel Mohrt?' (in French) (my editor of sorts there, a Breton from Lannion Bay at Louquarec.)

'He's out to lunch too.'

But the fact of the matter was, he was in New York that day but she couldnt care less to tell me and with me sitting in front of this imperious secretary who must've thought she was very Madame Defarge herself in Dickens' 'Tale of Two Cities' sewing the names of potential guillotine victims into the printer's cloth, were a half dozen eager or worried future writers with their manuscripts all of whom gave me a positively dirty look when they heard my name as tho they were muttering to themselves '*Kerouac*? I can write ten times better than that beatnik maniac and I'll prove it with this here manuscript called "Silence au Lips" all about how Renard walks into the foyer lighting a cigarette and refuses to acknowledge the sad formless smile of the plotless Lesbian heroine whose father just died trying to rape an elk in the Battle of Cuckamonga, and Philippe the intellectual enters in the next chapter lighting a cigarette with an existential leap across the blank page I leave next, all ending in a monologue encompassing etc., all this Kerouac can do is write stories, ugh' – 'And in such bad taste, not even one well-defined heroine in domino slacks crucifying chickens for her mother with hammer and nails in a "Happening" in the kitchen' – agh, all I feel like singing is Jimmy Lunceford's old tune:

> 'It aint watcha do
> It's the way atcha do it!'

But seeing the sinister atmosphere of 'literature' all around me and the broad aint gonna get my publisher to buzz me into his office for an actual business chat, I get up and snarl:

'Aw shit, *j'm'en va à l'Angleterre*' (Aw shit, I'm goin to England') but I should really have said:

'*Le Petit Prince s'en va à la Petite Bretagne.*'

Means: 'The Little Prince is going to Little Britain' (or, Brittany.)

17

Over at Gare St-Lazare I bought an Air-Inter ticket *one-way* to Brest (not heeding Goulet's advice) and cashed a travellers check of $50 (big deal) and went to my hotel room and spent two hours repacking so everything'd be alright and checking the rug on the floor for any lints I mighta left, and went down all dolled up (shaved etc.) and said goodbye to the evil woman and the nice man her husband who ran the hotel, with my hat on now, the rain hat I intended to wear on the midnight sea rocks, always wore it pulled down over the left eye I guess because that's the way I wore my pea cap in the Navy – There were no great outcries of please come back but the desk clerk observed me as tho he was like to try me sometime.

Off we go in the cab to Orly airfield, in the rain again, 10 A.M. now, the cab zipping with beautiful speed out past all those signs advertising cognac and the surprising little stone country houses in between with French gardens of flowers and vegetables exquisitely kept, everything green as I imagine it must be in Auld England now.

(Like a nut I figured I could fly from Brest to London, only 150 miles as the crow flies.)

At Orly I check in my small but heavy suitcase at Air-Inter and then wander around till 12 noon boarding call. I drink cognac and beer in the really marvelous cafes they have in that air terminal, nothing so dismal as Idlewild Kennedy with its plush-carpet and cocktail-lounge Everybody-Quiet shot. For the second time I give a franc to the lady who sits in front of the toilets at a table, asking her: 'Why do you sit there and why do people give you tips?'

'Because I *clean* the joint' which I understand right away and appreciate, thinking of my mother back home who has to *clean* the house while I yell insults at the TV from my rockingchair. So I say:

'*Un franc pour la Française.*'

I coulda said 'The Inferno White Owl Sainte Theresia!' and she still wouldna cared. (Wouldn't *have* cared, but I shorten things, after that great poet Robert Burns.)

So now it's 'Mathilda' I'm singing because the bell-tone announcing flights sings just like that song, in Orly, 'Ma – Thil – Daa' and the quiet girlvoice: 'Pan American Airlines Flight 603 to Karachi now loading at gate 32' or 'KLM Royal Dutch Airlines Flight 709 to Johannesburg now loading at gate 49' and so on, what an airport, people hear me singing 'Mathilda' all over the place and I've already had a long talk about dogs with two Frenchmen and a dachshund in the cafe, and now I hear: 'Air-Inter Flight 3 to Brest now loading at gate 96' and I start walking – down a long smooth corridor—

I walk about I swear a quartermile and come practically to the end of the terminal building and there's Air-Inter, a two-engined old B–26 I guess with worried mechanics all fiddling around the propeller on the port side—

It's flight time, noon, but I ask the people there 'What's wrong?'

'One hour delay.'

There's no toilet here, no cafe, so I go back all the way to while away the hour in a cafe, and wait—

I go back at one.

'Half hour delay.'

I decide to sit it out, but suddenly I have to go to the toilet at 1.20 – I ask a Spanish-looking Brest-bound passenger: 'Think I got time to go to the toilet back at the terminal?'

'O sure, plenty time.'

I look, the mechanics out there are still worriedly fiddling, so I hurry that quartermile back, to the toilet, lay another

franc for fun on La Française, and suddenly I hear 'Ma –
Thil – Daa' singsong with the word 'Brest' so I like Clark
Gable's best fast walk hike on back almost as fast as a
jogging trackman, if you know what I mean, but by the time
I get there the plane is out taxiing to the runway, the ramp's
been rolled back which all those traitors just crept up, and
off they go to Brittany with my suitcase.

18

Now I'm supposed to go dabbling all over France with clean fingernails and a joyous tourist expression.

'*Calvert*!' I blaspheme at the desk (for which I'm sorry, Oh Lord). 'I'm going to follow them in a train! Can you sell me a train ticket? They took off with my valise!'

'You'll have to go to Gare Montparnasse for that but I'm really sorry, Monsieur, but that is the most ridiculous way to miss a plane.'

I say to myself 'Yeah, you cheapskates, why dont you build a toilet.'

But I go in a taxi 15 miles back to Gare Montparnasse and I buy a one-way ticket to Brest, first class, and as I think about my suitcase, and what Goulet said, I also remember now the pirates of St Malo not to mention the pirates of Penzance.

Who cares? I'll catch up with the rats.

I get on the train among thousands of people, turns out there's a holiday in Brittany and everybody's going home.

There are those compartments where firstclass ticketed people can sit, and those narrow window alleys where secondclass ticketed people stand leaning at the windows and watch the land roll by – I pass the first compartment of the coach I picked and see nothing but women and babies – I know instinctively I'll choose the second compartment – And I do! Because what do I see in there but '*Le Rouge et le Noir*' (The Red and the Black), that is to say, the Military and the Church, a French soldier and a Catholic priest, and not only that but two pleasant looking old ladies and a weird looking drunklooking guy in the corner, that makes five, leaving the sixth and last place for me, 'Jean-Louis Lebris de

Kerouac' as I presently announce, knowing I'm home and they'll understand my family picked up some weird manners in Canada and the USA – which I announce of course only after I've asked '*Je peu m'assoir?*' (I can sit?), 'Yes,' and I excuse myself across the ladies' legs and plump right down next to the priest, removed my hat already, and address him: '*Bonjour, mon Père.*'

Now this is the real way to go to Brittany, gents.

19

But the poor little priest, dark, shall we say swart, or *swartz*, and very small and thin, his hands are trembling as if from ague and for all I know from Pascalian ache for the equation of the Absolute or maybe Pascal scared him and the other Jesuits with his bloody 'Provincial Letters', but in any case I look into his dark brown eyes, I see his weird little parroty understanding of everything and of me too, and I pound my collarbone with my finger and say:

'I'm Catholic too.'

He nods.

'I wear the Sacred Queen and also St Benedict.'

He nods.

He is such a little guy you could blow him away with one religious yell like '*O Seigneur*!' (Oh Lord!)

But now I turn my attention to the civilian in the corner, who's eyeing me with the exact eyes of an Irishman I know called Jack Fitzgerald and the same mad thirsty leer as tho he's about to say 'Alright, where's the booze hidden in that raincoat of yours' but all he does say is, in French:

'Take off your raincoat, put it up on the rack.'

Excusing myself as I have to bump knees with the blond soldier, and the soldier grins sadly ('cause I rode in trains with Aussies across wartime England 1943) I shove the lump of coat up, smile at the ladies, who just wanta get home the hell with all the characters, and I say my name to the guy in the corner (like I said I would).

'Ah, that's Breton. You live in Rennes?'

'No I live in Florida in America but I was born etc. etc.' the whole long story, which interests them, and then I ask the guy's name.

It's the beautiful name of Jean-Marie Noblet.

'Is that Breton?'

'*Mais oui.*' (But yes.)

I think: 'Noblet, Goulet, Havet, Champsecret, sure a lot of funny spellings in this country' as the train starts up and the priest settles down with a sigh and the ladies nod and Noblet eyes me like he would like to wink me a proposal that we get on with the drinking, a long trip ahead.

So I say 'Let's you and I go buy some in the *commissaire.*'

'If you wanta try, okay.'

'What's wrong?'

'Come on, you'll see.'

And sure enough we have to rush weaving without bumping anybody through seven coaches of packed windowstanders and on through the roaring swaying vestibules and jump over pretty girls sitting on books on the floor and avoid collisions with mobs of sailors and old country gentlemen and all the lot, a homecoming holiday train like the Atlantic Coast Line going from New York to Richmond, Rocky Mount, Florence, Charleston, Savannah and Florida on the Fourth of July or Christmas and everybody bringing gifts like Greeks beware we not of—

But me and old Jean-Marie find the liquor man and buy two bottles of rosé wine, sit on the floor awhile and chat with some guy, then catch the liquor man as he's coming back the other way and almost empty, buy two more, become great friends, and rush back to our compartment feeling great, high, drunk, wild – And don't you think we didnt swing infos back and forth in French, and not Parisian either, and him not speaking a word of English.

I didnt even have a chance to look out the window as we passed the Chartres Cathedral with the dissimilar towers one five hundred years older'n the other.

What gets me is that, after an hour Noblet and I were waving our wine bottles across the poor priest's face as we argued religion, history, politics, so suddenly I turned to him trembling there and asked: 'Do you mind our wine bottles?'

He gave me a look as if to say: 'You mean that lil ole winemaker me? No, no, I have a cold, you see, I feel awful sick.'

'Il est malade, il à un rheum,' (He's sick, he's got a cold) I told Noblet grandly. The Soldier was laughing all the while.

I said grandly to them all (and the English translation is beneath this):- *'Jésu à été crucifié parce que, a place d'amenez l'argent et le pouvoir, il à amenez seulement l'assurance que l'existence à été formez par le Bon Dieu et elle appartiens au Bon Dieu le Père, et Lui, le Père, va nous élever au Ciel après la mort, ou personne n'aura besoin d'argent ou de pouvoir parce que ça c'est seulement après tout d'la poussière et de la rouille – Nous autres qu'ils n'ont pas vue les miracles de Jésu, comme les Juifs et les Romans et la 'tites poignée d'Grecs et d'autres de la rivière Nile et Euphrates, on à seulement de continuer d'accepter l'assurance qu'il nous à été descendu dans la parole sainte du nouveau testament – C'est pareille comme ci, en voyant quelqu'un, on dira "c'est pas lui, c'est pas lui!" sans savoir QUI est lui, et c'est seulement le Fils qui connaient le Père – Alors, la Foi, et l'Église qui à dèfendu la Foi comme qu'a pouva.'* (Partly French Canuck.) IN ENGLISH:- 'Jesus was crucified because, instead of bringing money and power, He only brought the assurance that existence was created by God and it belongs to God the Father, and He, the Father, is going to elevate us to Heaven after death, where no one will need money or power because that's only after all dust and rust – We who have not seen the Miracles of Jesus, like the Jews and the Romans and the little handful of Greeks and others from the Nile River and the Euphrates, only have to continue accepting the assurance which has been handed down to us in the Holy Writ of the New Testament – It's just as though, on seeing someone, we'd say "It's not him, it's not him!" without knowing WHO he is, and it's only the Son who knows the Father – Therefore, Faith, and the Church which defended the Faith as well as it could.'

No applause from the priest, but a side underlook, brief, like the look of an applauder, thank God.

21

Was that my Satori, that look, or Noblet?

In any case it grew dark and when we got to Rennes, in Brittany now, and I saw soft cows out in the meadows dark blue near the rail, Noblet, against the advice of the *farceurs* (jokesters) of Paris advised me not to stay in the same coach, but change to three coaches ahead, because the trainmen were gonna make a cut and leave me right there (headed, really, however, for my real ancestral country, Cornouialles and environs) but the trick was to get to Brest.

He led me off the train, after the others, and walked me down the steaming station platform, stopped me at a liquor man so I could buy me a flask of cognac for the rest of the ride, and said goodbye: he was home, in Rennes, and so was the priest and the soldier, Rennes the former capital of all Brittany, seat of an Archbishop, headquarters of the 10th Army Corps, with the university and many schools, but not the real deep Brittany because in 1793 it was the headquarters of the Republican Army of the French Revolution against the Vendéans further in. And has ever since then been made the tribunal watchdog over those wild dog places. La Vendée, the name of the war between those two forces in history, was this:– the Bretons were against the Revolutionaries who were atheists and headcutters for fraternal reasons, while the Bretons had paternal reasons to keep to their old way of life.

Nothing to do with Noblet in 1965 AD.

He disappeared into the night like a Céline character but what's the use of similes when discussing a gentleman's departure, and high as a noble at that, but not as drunk as me.

We'd come 232 miles from Paris, had 155 to go to Brest (end, *finis*, land, *terre*, Finistère), all the sailors still on board the train as naturally, as I didnt know, Brest is a Naval Base where Chateaubriand heard the booming cannons and saw the fleet come in triumphant from some fight in 1770s sometime.

My new compartment is just a young mother with a cantankerous baby daughter, and some guy I guess her husband, and I just occasionally sip my cognac then go out in the alleyway to look out the window at passing darkness with lights, a lone granite farmhouse with lights on just downstairs in the kitchen, and vague hints of hills and moors.

Clickety clack.

I get pretty friendly with the young couple and at St Brieuc the trainman yells out 'Saint Brrieu!' – I yell out 'Saint Brieuck!'

Trainman, seeing nobody's getting much off or on, the lonely platform, repeats, advising me how to pronouce these Breton names: 'Saint Brrieu!'

'Saint Brieuck!' I yell, emphasizing as you see the 'c' noise of the thing there.

'Saint Brrieu!'

'Saint Brieuck!'

'Saint Brrieu!'

'Saint Brrieuck!'

'Saint Brrrieu!'

'Saint Brrrieuck!'

Here he realizes he's dealing with a maniack and quits the game with me and it's a wonder I didn't get thrown off the train right there on the wild shore here called Coasts of the North (Côtes du Nord) but he didnt even bother, after all the Little Prince had his firstclass ticket and Little Prick more likely.

But that was funny and I still insist, when you're in Brittany (Armorica the ancient name), land of Kelts, pronounce your 'K's' with a *kuck* – And as I've said elsewhere, if 'Celts' were pronounced with a soft 's' sound, as the Anglo-Saxons seem to do, my name would sound like this: (and other names):–

Jack Serouac

Johnny Sarson

Senator Bob Sennedy

Hopalong Sassidy
Deborah Serr (or Sarr)
Dorothy Silgallen
Mary Sarney
Sid Simpleton
   and the
      Stone Monuments of Sarnac via Sornwall.

And anyway there's a place in Cornwall called St Breock, and we all know how to pronounce that.

We finally arrive in Brest, end of the line, no more land, and I help the wife and husband out holding their portable crib thing – And there she is, grim misting fog, strange faces looking at the few passengers getting off, a distant hoot of a boat, and a grim cafe across the street where Lord I'll get no sympathy, I've come to trapdoor Brittany.

Cognacs, beers, and then I ask where's the hotel, right across the construction field – To my left, stone wall overlooking grass and sudden drops and dim houses – Foghorn out there – The Atlantic's bay and harbor—

Where's my suitcase? asks the desk man in the grim hotel, why it's in the air line office I guess—

No rooms.

Unshaven, in a black raincoat with rain hat, dirty, I walk outa there and go sploopsing up dark streets looking like any decent American Boy in trouble, old or young, for the Main Drag – I instantly recognize it for what it is, Rue de Siam, named after the King of Siam when he visited here on some dull visit certainly grim too and probably ran back to his tropical canaries as quick as he could since the new mason breastworks of Colbert certainly dont inspire no hope in the heart of a Buddhist.

But I'm not a Buddhist, I'm a Catholic revisiting the ancestral land that fought for Catholicism against impossible odds yet won in the end, as *certes*, at dawn, I'll hear the tolling of the *tocsin* churchbells for the dead.

I hit for the brightest looking bar on Rue de Siam which is a main street like the ones you used to see, say, in the 40s, in Springfield, Mass., or Redding, Calif., or that main street James Jones wrote about in 'Some Came Running' in Illinois—

The owner of the bar is behind his cash register doping out the horses at Longchamps – I immediately talk, tell him my name, his name is Mr Quéré (which reminds me of the spelling of Québec) and he lets me sit and goof and drink there all I want – Meanwhile the young bartender is also glad to talk to me, has apparently heard of my books, but after awhile (and just like Pierre LeMaire in La Gentilhommière) he suddenly stiffens, I guess from a sign from the boss, too much work to do, wash your glasses in the sink, I've outworn me welcome in another bar—

I've seen that expression on my father's face, a kind of disgusted lip-on-lip WHAT'S-THE-USE phooey, or ploof (dédain) or plah, as he either walked away a loser from the racetrack or out of a bar where he didn't like what happened, elsetimes, especially when thinking of history and the world, but that's when I walked out of that bar when that expression came over my own face – And the owner, who'd been really warm for a half hour, returned his attention to his figures with the sly underlook of after all a busy patron anywhere – But something had swiftly changed. (Gave my name for the first time.)

Their directions given to me for to find a hotel room did not evolve or *de*-volve me an actual brick and concrete place with a bed inside for me to lay my head in.

Now I was wandering in the very dark, in the fog, everything was closing down. Hoodlums roared by in small cars and some on motorcycles. Some stood on corners. I asked everybody where there was a hotel. Now they didnt even know. Gettin on 3 A.M. Groups of hoodlums came and went across the street from me. I say 'hoodlums' but with everything closed, the final music joint already discharging a few wrangling customers who bellowed confusedly around cars, what was left i' the streets?

Miraculously, yet, I suddenly passed a band of twelve or so Naval inductees who were singing a martial song in chorus on the foggy corner. I went right up to em, looked at the head singer, and with me alcoholic hoarse baritone went 'Aaaaaah' – They waited—

'Véééé'

They wondered who this nut was

'Mah – reeeee – ee – ee – aaaah!'

Ah, *Ave Maria*, on the next notes I knew not the words but just sang the melody and they caught on, caught up the tune, and there we were a chorus of baritone and tenors singing like sad angels suddenly slowly – And right through the whole first chorus – In the foggy foggy dew – Brest Brittany – Then I said 'Adieu' and walked away. They never said a word.

Some nut with a raincoat and a hat.

23

Well, why do people change their names? Have they done anything bad, are they criminals, are they ashamed of their real names? Are they afraid of something? Is there any law in America against using your own real name?

I had come to France and Brittany just to look up this old name of mine which is just about three thousand years old and was never changed in all that time, as who would change a name that simply means House (Ker), In the Field (Ouac)—

Just as you say Camp (Biv), In the Field (Ouac) (unless 'bivouac' is the incorrect spelling of an old Bismarck word, silly to say that because 'bivouac' was a word used long before 1870 Bismarck) – the name Kerr, or Carr, simply means *House*, why bother with a field?

I knew that the name of Cornish Celtic Language is Kernauk. I knew that there are stone monuments called dolmens (tables of stone) at Kériaval in Carnac, some called alignments at Kermario, Kérlescant and Kérdouadec, and a town nearby called Kéroual, and I knew that the original name for Bretons was 'Breons' (i.e. the Breton is *Le Breon*) and that I had an additive name 'Le Bris' and here I was in 'Brest' and did this make me a Cimbric spy from the stone monuments of Riestedt in Germany? Rietstap also the name of the German who painstakingly compiled names of families and their scocheons and had my family included in 'Rivista Araldica'? – You say I'm a snob – I only wanted to find out why my family never changed their name and perchance find a tale there, and trace it back to Cornwall, Wales, and Ireland and maybe Scotland afore that I'm sure, then down over to the St Lawrence River city in Canada where I'm told there was a Seigneurie (a Lordship) and therefore I can go live there (along with my thousands of bowlegged French Canadian cousins bearing the same name) and *never pay taxes*!

Now what redblooded American with a Pontiac, a big mortgage and ulcers at March-time is not interested in this great adventure!

Hey! I should've also sang to the Navy boys:

> 'I joined the Navy
> To see the world
> And whaddid I see?
> I saw the sea.'

24

Now I'm getting scared, I suspect some of those guys crisscrossing the streets in front of my wandering path are fixing to mug me for my two or three hundred bucks left – It's foggy and still except for the sudden squeek wheels of cars loaded with guys, no girls now – I get mad and go up to an apparent elderly printer hurrying home from work or cardgame, maybe my father's ghost, as surely as my father musta looked down on me that night in Brittany at last where he and all his brothers and uncles and their fathers had all longed to go, and only poor Ti Jean finally made it and poor Ti Jean with his Swiss Army knife in the suitcase locked in an airfield twenty miles away across the moors – He, Ti Jean, threatened now not by Bretons, as on those tourney mornings when flags and public women made fight an honorable thing I guess, but in Apache alleys the slur of Wallace Beery and worse than that of course, a thin mustache and a thin blade or a small nickel plated gun – No garrottes please, I've got my armor on, my Reichian character armor that is – How easy to joke about it as I scribble this 4,500 miles away safe at home in old Florida with the doors locked and the Sheriff doin his best in a town at least as bad but not as foggy and so dark—

I keep looking over my shoulder as I ask the printer 'Where are the gendarmes?'

He hurries past me thinking it's just a lead-in question to mug him.

On Rue de Siam I ask a young guy '*Ou sont les gendarmes, leurs offices?*' (Where are the gendarmes, their office?)

'Dont you want a cab?' (in French)

'To go where? There are no hotels?'

'The police station is down Siam here, then left and you'll see it.'

'Merci, Monsieur.'

I go down believing he gave me another bum steer as he's in cahoots with the hoodlums, I turn left, look over my shoulder, things have gotten suddenly mighty quiet, and I see a building blurring lights in the fog, the back of it, that I figure is the police station.

I listen. Not a sound anywhere. No screeching tires, no mumble voices, no sudden laughs.

Am I crazy? Crazy as that raccoon in Big Sur Woods, or the sandpiper thereof, or any Olsky-Polsky Sky Bum, or Route Sixty Six Silly Elephant Eggplant Sycophant and with more to come.

I walk right into the precinct, take my American green passport from out my breast pocket, present it to the gendarme desk sergeant and tell him I cannot wander these streets all night without a room, etc., have money for a room etc., suitcase locked up etc., missed my plane etc., am a tourist etc. and I am afearéd.

He understood.

His boss came out, the lieutenant I guess, they made a few calls, got a car out in front, I stuck 50 francs at the desk sergeant saying 'Merci beaucoup.'

He shook his head.

It was one of the only three bills I had left in my pocket (50 francs is worth $10) and when I reached into my pocket I thought maybe it was one of the 5 franc notes, or a ten, in any case the fifty came out like when you draw a card anyway, and I felt ashamed to think I was trying to bribe them, it was only a tip – But you dont 'tip' the police of France.

In fact this *was* the Republican Army defending a descendant of the Vendéan Bretons caught without his trapdoor.

Like the 20 centimes in St Louis de France that I shoulda stuck in the poorbox, as gold of the real Caritas, I really could have dropped it on the stationhouse floor as I went out but how can such a thought spontaneously enter the head of a crafty worthless Canuck like me?

Or if the thought had entered my mind, would they cry bribe?

No – the Gendarmes of France have a school of their own.

25

This cowardly Breton (me) watered down by two centuries in Canada and America, nobody's fault but my own, this Kerouac who would be laughed at in Prince of Wales Land because he cant even hunt, or fish, or fight a beef for his fathers, this boastful, this prune, this rage and rake and rack of lacks, 'this trunk of humours' as Shakespeare said of Falstaff, this false staff not even a prophet let alone a knight, this fear-of-death tumor, with tumescences in the bathroom, this runaway slave of football fields, this strikeout artist and base thief, this yeller in Paris salons and mum in Breton fogs, this farceur jokester at art galleries of New York and whimperer at police stations and over longdistance telephones, this prude, this yellowbellied aide-de-camp with portfolio full of port and folios, this pinner of flowers and mocker at thorns, this very *Hurracan* like the gasworks of Manchester and Birmingham both, this ham, this tester of men's patience and ladies' panties, this boneyard of decay eating at rusty horse shoes hoping to win a game from . . . This, in short, scared and humbled dumbhead loudmouth with-the-shits descendant of man.

The gendarmes have a school of their own, meaning, they dont accept bribes or tips, they say with their eyes: 'To each his own, you with your fifty francs, me with my honorable civic courage – and civil at that.'

Boom, he drives me to a little Breton inn on Rue Victor Hugo.

26

A haggard guy like any Irishman comes out and tightens his
bathrobe at the door, listens to the gendarmes, okay, leads
me into the room next to the desk which I guess is where guys
bring their girls for a quickie, unless I'm wrong and taking
off again on joking about life – The bed is perfect with
seventeen layers of blankets over sheets and I sleep for three
hours and suddenly they're yelling and scrambling for
breakfast again with shouts across courtyards, bing, bang,
clatter of pots and shoes dropping on the second floor, cocks
crowing, it's France and morning—

I gotta see it and anyway I cant sleep and where's my
cognac!

I wash my teeth with my fingers at the little sink and rub
my hair with my fingertips wishing I had my suitcase and
step out in the inn like that looking for the toilet naturally.
There's old Innkeeper, actually a young guy 35 and a Breton,
I forgot or omitted to ask his name, but he doesnt care how
wildhaired I am and that the gendarmes had to find me a
room, 'There's the toilet, first right.'

'La Poizette ah?' I yell.

He gives me the look that says 'Get in the toilet and shut
up.'

When I come out I am trying to get to my sink in my room
to comb my hair but he's already got breakfast coming for
me in the diningroom where nobody is but us—

'Wait, comb my hair, get my cigarettes, and, ah, how
about a beer first?'

'Wa? You crazy? Have your coffee first, your bread and
butter.'

'Just a little beer.'

'AWright, awright, just one – Sit here when you get back, I've got work to do in the kitchen.'

But this is all spoken that fast and even, but in Breton French which I dont have to make an effort like I do in Parisian French, to enunciate: just: '*Ey, weyondonc, pourquoi t'a peur que j'm'dégrise avec une 'tite bierre?*' (Hey, come on, how come you're scared of me sobering up with a little beer?)

'*On s'dégrise pas avec la bierre, Monsieur, mais avec le bon petit déjeuner.*' (We dont sober up with beer, Monsieur, but with a nice breakfast.)

'*Way, mais on est pas toutes des soulons.*' (Yah, but not everybody's a drunk.)

'Dont talk like that Monsieur. It's there, look, here, in the good Breton butter made with cream, and bread fresh from the baker, and strong hot coffee, that's how we sober up – Here's your beer, voila, I'll keep the coffee hot on the stove.'

'Good! Now there's a real man.'

'You speak the good French but you have an accent—?'

'*Oua, du Canada.*'

'Ah yes, because your passport is American.'

'But I havent learned French in books but at home, I didnt know how to speak English in America before I was, oh, five six years old, my parents were born in Canada in Québec, the name of my mother is L' Évêque.'

'Ah, that's Breton also.'

'But why, I thought it was Norman.'

'Well Norman, Breton—'

'This and that – the French of the North in any case, ahn?'

'*Ah oui.*'

I pour myself a creamlike head over my beer out of the bottle of Alsatian beer, the best i' the west, as he watches disgusted, in his apron, he has rooms to clean upstairs, what's this dopey American Canuck hanging him up for and why does this always happen to him?

I say to him my full name and he yawns and says '*Way,*

there are a lot of Lebris' here in Brest, coupla dozen. This morning before you got up a party of Germans had a great breakfast right where you're sittin there, they're gone now.'

'They had fun in Brest?'

'*Cer*tainly! You've got to stay! You only got here yesterday—'

'I'm going to Air-Inter get my valise and I'm going to England, today.'

'But' – he looks at me helplessly – 'you havent seen Brest!'

I said 'Well, if I can come back here tonight and sleep I can stay in Brest, after all I've gotta have *some* place' ('I may not be an experienced German tourist,' I add to think to myself, 'not having toured Brittany in 1940 but I certainly know some boys in Massachusetts who toured it for you outa the St Lo breakthrough in 1944, I do') ('and French Canadian boys at that.') – And that's that, because he says:-

'Well I may not have a room for you tonight, and then again I may, all depends, Swiss parties are coming.'

('And Art Buchwald,' I thought.)

He said: 'Now eat your good Breton butter.' The butter was in a little clay bucket two inches high and so wide and so cute I said:-

'Let me have this butter bucket when I've finished the butter, my mother will love it and it will be a souvenir for her from Brittany.'

'I'll get you a clean one from the kitchen. Meanwhile you eat your breakfast and I'll go upstairs and make a few beds' so I slup down the rest of the beer, he brings the coffee and rushes upstairs, and I smur (like Van Gogh's butterburls) fresh creamery butter outa that little bucket, almost all of it in one bite, right on the fresh bread, and crunch, munch, talk about your Fritos, the butter's gone even before Krupp and Remington got up to stick a teaspoon smallsize into a butler-cut-up grapefruit.

Satori there in Victor Hugo Inn?

When he comes down, nothing's left but me and one of those wild powerful Gitane (means Gypsy) cigarettes and smoke all over.

'Feel better?'

'Now that's butter – the bread extraspecial, the coffee strong and exquisite – But now I desire my cognac.'

'Well pay your room bill and go down rue Victor Hugo, on the corner is cognac, go get your valise and settle your affairs and come back here find out if there's a room tonight, beyond that old buddy old Neal Cassady cant go no further. To each his own and I got a wife and kids upstairs so busy playing with flowerpots, if, why if I had a thousand Syrians racking the place in Nominoé's own brown robes, they'd still let me do all the work, as it is, as you know, a hard-net Keltic sea.' (I ingrained his thought there for your delectation, and if you didnt like it, call it beanafaction, in other words I beaned ya with my high hard one.)

I say 'Where's Plouzaimedeau? I wanta write poems by the side of the sea at night.'

'Ah you mean Plouzémédé – Ah, spoff, not my affair – I gotta work now.'

'Okay I'll go.'

But as an example of a regular Breton, aye?

27

So I go down to the corner bar as directed and walk in and
there's old Papa Bourgeois or more likely Kervélégan or
Ker-thisser and Ker-thatter behind the bar, gives me a cold
gyrene look gyring me wide around and I say 'Cognac,
Monsieur.' He takes his bloody time. A young mailman
walks in with his leather shoulder-hanging pouch and starts
in talking to him. I take my delicate cognac to a table and sit
and on the first sip I shudder to miss what I missed all night.
(They had some brands there besides Hennessey and
Courvoisier and Monnet, that musta been why Winston
Churchill that old Baron crying for his hounds in his weird
wield weir, was always in France with cigar-a-mouth
painting.) The owner eyes me narrowly. Clearly. I go up to
the mailman and say: 'Where's the office in town of the Air-
Inter airplane company?'

'No savvy' (but in French).

'You a mailman in Brest and dont even know where an
important office is?'

'What's so important about it?'

('Well for one thing,' I say to myself to him extra-
sensorily, 'it's the only way you can get outa here – *fast*.') But
all I say is: 'My suitcase is there and I'm gonna get it back.'

'Gee I dont know where it is. Do *you*, boss?'

No answer.

I said 'Okay, I'll find it myself' and finished my cognac,
and the mailman said:

'I am only a *facteur*' (mailman).

I said something to him in French which is published in
heaven, which I insist to print here only in French: '*Tu
travaille avec la maille pi tu sais seulement pas s'qu'est une
office – d'importance?*'

'I'm new on the job' he said in French.

I'm not trying to belabor no point but listen to this:–

It's not my fault, or that of any American tourist or even patriot, that the French refuse the responsibility of their explanations – It's their right to demand privacy, but farcing is submittable to a court of Law, O Monsieur Bacon et Monsieur Coke – Farcing, or deceit, is submittable to a court of Law when it concerns your loss of civil welfare or safety.

It's as tho some Negro tourist like Papa Kane of Senegal came up to me on the sidewalk on Sixth Avenue and 34th Street and asked me which way to the Dixie Hotel on Times Square, and instead I directed him to the Bowery, where he would (let's say) be killed by Basque and Indian muggers, and a witness heard me give this innocent African tourist these wrong directions, and then testified in court that he heard these *farcing* instructions with intent to deprive of right-of-way, or right-of-social-way, or right-of-proper-*direction*, then let's blast all the uncooperative and unmannerly divisionist rats on both sides of Spoofism and other Isms too anyway.

But the old owner of the bar quietly tells me where it is and I thank him and go.

28

Now I see the harbor, the flowerpots in back of kitchens, old Brest, the boats, coupla tankers out there, and the wild headlands in the gray scudding sky, summat like Nova Scotia.

I find the office and go in. Here's two characters in there involved with onionskinned duplicated copies of everything and not even a mistress on their knee, tho she's in back right now. I put points, papers, down, they say wait an hour. I say I wanta fly to London tonight. They say Air-Inter doesnt fly direct to London but back to Paris and you gets another company. ('Brest is only a you-know-what-hair from Cornwall,' I wish I could tell them, 'why fly back to Paris?') 'Alright, so I'll fly to Paris. What time today?'

'Not today. Monday is the next flight from Brest.'

I can just picture myself hanging around Brest for one jolly whole weekend with no hotel room and no one to talk to. Right then a gleam comes in my eye as I think: 'It's Saturday morning, I can be in Florida in time for the funnies at dawn when the guy placks em on my driveway!' – 'Is there a train back to Paris?'

'Yes, at three.'

'Sell me a ticket?'

'You have to go there yourself.'

'And my suitcase again?'

'Wont be here till noon.'

'So I go buy ticket at railroad station, talk to Stepin Fetchit awhile and call him Old Black Joe, and even sing it, give him French kiss, peck on each cheek, give him quarter, and come back here.'

I didnt actually say that but I shoulda but I only said

'Okay' and went down the station, got the firstclass ticket, came back the same way, by now already an expert on Brest streets, looked in, no suitcase yet, went to Rue de Siam, cognac and beer, dull, came back, no suitcase, so went into the bar next door to this Air Office of the Breton Air Force which I should write long letters to MacMullen of SAC about—

I know there are a lot of beautiful churches and chapels out there that I should go look at, and then England, but since England's in my heart why go there? and 'sides, it doesnt matter how charming cultures and art are, they're useless without sympathy – All the prettiness of tapestries, lands, people:– *worthless* if there is no sympathy – Poets of genius are just decorations on the wall if without the poetry of kindness and Caritas – This means that Christ was right and everybody since then (who 'thought' and wrote opposing views of their own) (like, say, Sigmund Freud and his cold depreciation of helpless personalities), was *wrong* – in that, the life of a person is, as W. C. Fields says, 'Fraught with eminent peril' but when you know that when you die you will be elevated because you've done no harm, Ah take that back to Brittany and Elsewhere too – Do we need a Definition-of-Harm University to teach this? Let no man impel you to evil. The Guardian of Purgatory has the two Keys to St Peter's Gate and himself's the third and deciding key.

And you impel no one to evil, or you shall have the balls of your eyes and the rest roasted like at an Iroquois stake and by the Devil himself, he who chose Judas for his chews. (Outa Dante.)

Whatever wrong you do shall be returned to you a hundredfold, jot and tittle, by the laws that operate in what science now calls 'the deepening mystery of research.'

Well re-search this, Creighton, by the time yore investigations are complete, the Hound Dog of Heaven'll take you straight to Massah.

29

So I go into that bar so's not to miss my suitcase with its blessed belongings, as if like Joe E. Lewis the comedian I could try to take my things to Heaven with me, while you're alive on earth the very hairs of your cats on your clothes are blessed, and later on we can all gape and yaw at Dinosaurs together, well, here's this bar and I go in, sip awhile, go back two doors, the suitcase's there at last and tied to a chain.

The clerks say nothing, I pick up the suitcase and the chain falls off. Naval cadets in there buying tickets stare as I lift the suitcase. I show them my name written in orange paint on a black tape strip near the keyhole. My name. I walk out, with it.

I lug the suitcase into Fournier's bar and stash it in the corner and sit at the bar, feeling my railroad tickets, and have two hours to drink and wait.

The name of the place is Le Cigare.

Fournier the owner comes in, only 35, and right away gets on the phone going like this: 'Allo, oui, cinque, yeh, quatre, yeh, deux, bon,' bang the phone hook. I realize it's a bookie joint.

O then I tell them joyously 'And who do you think is the best jockey today in America? Hah?'

As if they cared.

'Turcotte!' I yell triumphantly. 'A Frenchman! Dint you see him win that Preakness?'

Preakness, Shmeakness, they never even heard of it, they've got the Grand Prix de Paris to worry about not to mention the Prix du Conseil Municipal and the Prix Gladiateur and the St Cloud and Maisons Lafitte and Auteuil tracks, and Vincennes too, I gape to think what a big world this is that international horseplayers let alone pool players cant even get together.

But Fournier's real nice to me and says 'We had a couple French Canadians in here last week, you shoulda been here, they left their cravats on the wall: see em? They had a guitar and sang *turlutus* and had a *big* time.'

'Remember their names?'

'Nap – But you, American passport, Lebris de Kerouac you say, and came here to find news of your family, why you leaving Brest in a few hours?'

'Well, – now *you* tell me.'

'Seems to me' (*'me semble'*) 'if you made that much of an effort to come all the way out here, and all the trouble getting here, thru Paris and the libraries you say, now that you're here, it would be a shame if you didnt at least call up and go see *one* of the Lebris in this phone book – Look, there's dozens of em here. Lebris the pharmacist, Lebris the lawyer, Lebris the judge, Lebris the wholesaler, Lebris the restaurateur, Lebris the book dealer, Lebris the sea captain, Lebris the pediatrician—'

'Is there a Lebris who's a gynecologist who loves women's thighs?' (*'Ya ta un Lebris qu'est un gynecologiste qui aime les cuisses des femmes?'*) yell I, and everybody in the bar, including Fournier's barmaid, and the old guy on the stool beside me, naturally, *laugh*.

'—Lebris – hey, no jokes – Lebris the banker, Lebris of the Tribunal, Lebris the mortician, Lebris the importer—'

'Call up Lebris the restaurateur and I'll give *my* cravat.' And I take my blue knit rayon necktie off and hand it to him and open my collar like I'm at home. 'I cant understand these French telephones,' I add, and add to myself: ('But O you sure do' because I'm reminded of my great buddy in America who sits on the edge of his bed from first race to ninth race, butt in mouth, but not a big romantic smoking Humphrey Bogart butt, it's just an old Marlboro tip, brown and burnt-out from yesterday, and he's so fast on the phone

72

he might bite flies if they dont get outa the way, as soon's he picks up the phone it's not even rung yet but somebody's talking to him: 'Allo Tony? That'll be four, six, three, for a fin.')

Who ever thought that in my quest for ancestors I'd end up in a bookie joint in Brest, O Tony? brother of my friend?

Anyway Fournier does get on the phone, gets Lebris the restaurateur, has me use my most elegant French getting meself invited, hangs up, holds up his hands, and says: 'There, go see this Lebris.'

'Where are the ancient Kerouacs?'

'Probably in Cornouialles country at Quimper, somewhere in Finistère south of here, he'll tell you. My name is Breton also, why get excited?'

'It's not *every* day.'

'So *nu*?' (more or less). 'Excuse me' and the phone rings. 'And take back your necktie, it's a nice tie.'

'Is Fournier a Breton name?'

'Why shore.'

'What the hell,' I yelled, 'everybody's suddenly a Breton! Havet – LeMaire – Gibon – Fournier – Didier – Goulet – L'Évêque – Noblet – Where's old Halmalo, and the old Marquis de Lantenac, and the little Prince of Kérouac, *Çiboire, j'pas capable trouvez ca*—' (*Çiborium*, I cant find that).

'Just like the horses?' says Fournier. 'No! The lawyers in the little blue berets have changed all that. Go see Monsieur Lebris. And dont forget, if you come back to Brittany and Brest, come on over here with your friends, or your mother – or your cousins – But now the telephone is ringing, excuse me, Monsieur.'

So I cut outa there carrying that suitcase down the Rue de Siam in broad daylight and it weighs a ton.

73

30

Now starts another adventure. It's a marvellous restaurant just like Johnny Nicholson's in New York City, all marble-topped tables and mahogany and statuary, but very small, and here, instead of guys like Al and others rushing around in tight pants serving table, are girls. But they are the daughters and friends of the owner, Lebris. I come in and say where's Mr Lebris, I been invited. They say wait here and they go off and check, upstairs. Finally it's okay and I carry my suitcase up (feeling they didnt even believe me in the first place, those gals) and I'm shown a bedroom where lies a sharpnosed aristocrat in bed in mid day with a huge bottle of cognac at his side, plus I guess cigarettes, a comforter as big as Queen Victoria on top of his blankets (a comforter, that is, I mean a six-by-six *pillow*), and his blond doctor at the foot of the bed advising him how to rest – 'Sit down here' but even as that's happening a *romancier de police* walks in, that is, a writer of detective novels, wearing neat steel-rimmed spectacles and himself as clean as the pin o Heaven, with his charming wife – But then in walks poor Lebris' wife, a superb brunette (mentioned to me by Fournier) and three *ravissantes* (ravishing) girls who turn out to be one wed and two unwed daughters – And there I am being handed a cognac by Monsieur Lebris as he painstakingly raises himself from his heap of delicious pillows (O Proust!) and says to me liltingly:

'You are Jean-Louis Lebris de Kérouac, you said and they said on the phone?'

'*Sans doute, Monsieur.*' I show him my passport which says: 'John Louis Kerouac' because you cant go around America and join the Merchant Marine and be called 'Jean'.

But Jean is the man's name for John, *Jeanne* is the woman's name, but you cant tell that to your Bosun on the SS Robert Treat Paine when the harbor pilot calls on you to man the wheel through the mine nets and says at your side 'Two fifty one steady as you go.'

'Yes sir, two fifty one steady as I go.'

'Two fifty, steady as you go.'

'Two fifty, steady as I go.'

'Two fifty nine, steady, steady-y-y as you go' and we go glidin right amongst them mine nets, and into haven. (Norfolk 1944, after which I jumped ship.) Why did the pilot pick old Keroach? (Keroac'h, early spelling hassle among my uncles). Because Keroach has a steady hand you buncha rats who cant write let alone read books—

So my name on the passport is 'John' and was once Shaun when O'Shea and I done Ryan in and Murphy laughed and all we done Ryan in, was a pub.

'And your name?' I ask.

'Ulysse Lebris.'

Over the pillow comforter was the genealogical chart of his family, part of which is called Lebris de Loudéac, which he'd apparently called for preparatorily for my arrival. But he's just had a hernia operation, that's why he's in bed, and his doctor is concerned and telling him to do what should be done, and then leaves.

At first I wonder 'Is he Jewish? pretending to be a French aristocrat?' because something about him looks Jewish at first, I mean the particular racial type you sometimes see, pure *skinny* Semitic, the serpentine forehead, or shall we say, aquiline, and that long nose and funny hidden Devil's Horns where his baldness starts at the sides, and surely under that blanket he must have long thin feet (unlike my thick short fat peasant's feet) that he must waddle aside to aside *gazotsky* style, i.e., stuck out and walking on heels instead of front soles – And his foppish delightful airs, his Watteau fragrance, his Spinoza eye, his Seymour Glass (or Seymour

75

Wyse) elegance tho I then realize I've never seen anybody who looked like that except at the end of a lance in another lifetime, a regular *blade* who took long coach trips from Brittany to Paris maybe with Abelard to just watch bustles bounce under chandeliers, had affairs in rare cemeteries, grew sick of the city and returned to his evenly distributed trees thru which at least his mount knew how to canter, trot, gallop or take off – A coupla stone walls between Combourg and Champsecret, what matters it? A real *elegant—*

Which I told him right off, still studying his face to see if he was Jewish, but no, his nose was as gleeful as a razor, his blue eyes languid, his Devil's Horns out-and-out, his feet out of sight, his French diction perfectly clear to anybody even old Carl Adkins of West Virginia if he'd been there, every word meant to be understood, Ah me, to meet an old noble Breton, like tell that old Gabriel de Montgomeri the joke is over – For a man like this armies would form.

It's that old magic of the Breton noble and of the Breton genius, of which Master Matthew Arnold said: 'A note of Celtic extraction, which reveals some occult quality in a familiar object, or tinges it, one knows not how, with "the light that never was on sea or land."'

31

Kudos ever, but over, we begin a lick of conversation –
(Again, dear Americans of the land of my birth, in ratty
French comparable in context to the English they speak in
Essex):– Me:– 'Ah sieur, shite, one more cognac.'

''Ere you are, mighty.' (A pun on 'matey' there and let me
ask you but one more question, reader:- Where else but in a
book can you go back and catch what you missed, and not
only that but savor it and keep it up and shove it? D'any
Aussie ever tell you that?)

I say: 'But my, you are an elegant character, hey what?'
No answer, just a bright glance.

I feel like a clod has to explain himself. I gaze on him. His
head is turned parrotwise at the novelist and the ladies. I
notice a glint of interest in the novelist's eyes. Maybe he's a
cop since he writes police novels. I ask him across the pillows
if he knows Simenon? And has he read Dashiell Hammett,
Raymond Chandler and James M. Cain, not to mention B.
Traven?

I could better go into long serious controversies with M
Ulysse Lebris did he read Nicholas Breton of England, John
Skelton of Cambridge, or the ever-grand Henry Vaughan
not to mention George Herbert – and you could add, or
John Taylor the Water-Poet of the Thames?

Me and Ulysse cant even get a word in edgewise thru our
own thoughts.

32

But I'm home, there's no doubt about it, except if I were to want a strawberry, or loosen Alice's shoetongue, old Herrick in his grave *and* Ulysse Lebris would both yell at me to leave things alone, and that's when I raw my wide pony and roll.

Well, Ulysse then turns to me bashfully and just looks into my eyes briefly, and then away, because he knows no conversation is possible when every Lord and his blessed cat has an opinion on *everything*.

But he looks and says 'Come over and see my genealogy' which I do, dutifully, I mean, I cant see any more anyhow, but with my finger I trace a hundred old names indeed branching out in every direction, all Finistère and also Côtes du Nord and Morbihan names.

Now think for a minute of these three names:–

      (1) Behan
      (2) Mahan
      (3) Morbihan

Han? (for 'Mor' only means 'Sea' in Breton Celtic.)

I search blindly for that old Breton name Daoulas, of which 'Duluoz' was a variation I invented just for fun in my writerly youth (to use as my name in my novels).

'Where is the record of your family?' snaps Ulysse.

'In the Rivistica Heraldica!' I yell, when I shoulda said 'Rivista Araldica' which are Italian words meaning: 'Heraldic Review.'

He writes it down.

His daughter comes in again and says she's read some of my books, translated and published in Paris by that publisher who was out for lunch, and Ulysse is surprised. In fact his daughter wants my autograph. In fact I'm very Jerry Lewis himself in Heaven in Brittany in Israel getting high with Malachiah.

33

All joking aside, M Lebris was, and is, yair, an ace – I even
went so far as to help myself, to myself's own invitation (but
with a polite (?) eh?) to a third cognac, which at the time I
thought had mortified the *romancier de police* but he never
even glanced my way as tho he was studying marks of my
fingernails on the floor – (or lint)—

The fact of the matter is (again that cliché, but we need
signposts), me and M Lebris talked a blue streak about
Proust, de Montherlant, Chateaubriand, (where I told
Lebris he had the same nose), Saskatchewan, Mozart, and
then we talked of the futility of Surrealism, the loveliness of
loveliness, Mozart's flute, even Vivaldi's, by God I even
mentioned Sebastian del Piombo and how he was even more
languid than Raffaelo, and he countered with the pleasures
of a good comforter (at which point I reminded him
paranoiacally of the Paraclete), and he went on, expounding
'pon the glories of Armorica (ancient name of Brittany, *ar*,
'on', *mor*, 'the sea',) and I then told him with a dash of
thought:– or hyphen:– '*C'est triste de trouver que vous êtes
malade, Monsieur Lebris*' (pronounced Lebriss), 'It's sad to
find that you're ill, Monsieur Lebris, but joyous to find that
you're encircled by your lovers, truly, in whose company I
should always want to be found.'

This is all in fancy French and he answered 'That's well
put, and with eloquence *and* elegance, in a manner not
always understood nowadays' (and here we sorta winked at
each other as we realized we were going to start a routine of
talking like two overblown mayors or archbishops, just for
fun and to test my formal French), 'and it doesnt disturb me

to say, in front of my family and my friends, that you are the equal of the idol who has given you your inspiration' (*que vous êtes l'égale de l'idole qui vous à donnez votre inspiration*), 'if that thought is any comfort to you, you who, doubtless, have no need of comfort among those who wait upon you.'

Picking up: 'But, *certes*, Monsieur, your words, like the flowered barbs of Henry Fifth of England addressed to the poor little French princess, and right in front of his, Oh me, *her* chaperone, not as if to cut but as the Greeks say, the sponge of vinegar in the mouth was not a cruelty but (again, as we know on the Mediterranean sea) a shot that kills the thirst.'

'Well of course, expressed that way, I shall have no more words, but, in my feebleness to understand the extent of my vulgarities, but that is to say supported by your faith in my undignified efforts, the dignity of our exchange of words is understood surely by the cherubs, but that's not enough, *dignity* is such an exe-crable word, and now, before – but no I havent lost the line of my ideas, Monsieur Kerouac, he, in his excellence, and that excellence which makes me forget all, the family, the house, the establishment, in any case:– a sponge of vinegar *kills* the thirst?'

'Say the Greeks. And, if I could continue to explain everything that I know, your ears would lose the otiose air they wear now – You have, dont interrupt me, listen—'

'Otiose! A word for the Chief Inspector Charlot, dear Henri!'

The French detective story writer's not interested in my otiose or my odious nuther, but I'm trying to give you a stylish reproduction of how we talked and what was going on.

I sure hated to leave that sweet bedside.

Besides, lots of brandy there, as tho I couldnt go out and buy my own.

When I told him the motto of my ancestral family, '*Aimer,*

Travailler et Souffrir' (Love, Work and Suffer) he said: 'I like the *Love* part, as for Work it gave me hernia, and Suffer you see me now.'

Goodbye, Cousin!

P.S. (And the shield was: 'Blue with gold stripes accompanied by three silver nails.')

In sum: In 'Armorial Général de J. B. Riestap, Supplement par V. H. Rolland: LEBRIS DE KEROACK – Canada, originaire de Bretagne. D'azur au chevron d'or accompagné de 3 clous d'argent. D:– AIMER, TRA-VAILLER ET SOUFFRIR. RIVISTA ARALDICA, IV, 240.'

And old Lebris de Loudéac he shall certainly see Lebris de Kéroack again, unless one of us, or both of us, die – Which I remind my readers goes back to: Why change your name unless you're ashamed of something.

34

But I got so fascinated by old de Loudéac, and not one taxi outside on Rue de Siam, I had to hurry with that 70 pound suitcase in my paw, switching it from paw to paw, and missed my train to Paris by, count it, three minutes.

And I had to wait eight hours till eleven in the cafes around the station – I told the yard switchmen: 'You mean to tell me I missed that Paris train by *three* minutes? What are you Bretons tryna do, *keep* me here?' I went over to the deadend blocks and pressed against the oiled cylinder to see if it would give and it did so now at least I could write a letter (that'll be the day) back to Southern Pacific railroad brakemen now train masters and oldheads that in France they couple different, which I s'pose sounds like a dirty postcard, but it's true, but dingblast it I've lost ten pounds running from Ulysse Lebris' restaurant to the station (one mile) with that bag, alright, shove it, I'll store the bag in baggage and drink for eight hours—

But, as I unpin my little McCrory suitcase (Monkey Ward it actually was) key, I realize I'm too drunk and mad to open the lock (I'm looking for my tranquilizers which you must admit I need by now), in the suitcase, the key is pinned as according to my mother's instructions to my clothes – For a full twenty minutes I kneel there in the baggage station of Brest Brittany trying to make the little key open the snaplock, cheap suitcase anyhow, finally in a Breton rage I yell *'Ouvre donc maudit!'* (OPEN UP DAMN YOU!!) and break the lock – I hear laughter – I hear someone say: 'Le roi Kerouac' (the king Kerouac). I'd heard that from the wrong mouths in America. I take off the blue knit rayon necktie and, after taking out a pill or two, and an odd flask of cognac, I press down on the suitcase with the broken lock (one of em broken) and I wrap the necktie around, make one full twist tight, pull tight, and then, grabbing one end of the necktie in my teeth and pulling whilst holding the knot down with middle (or woolie) finger, I endeavor to bring the other end of the necktie around the taut toothpulled end, loop it in, steady as you go, then lower my great grinning teeth to the suitcase of all Brittany, till I'm kissing it, and *bang!*, mouth pulls one way, hand the other, and that thing is tied tighter than a tied-ass mother's everloving son, or son of a bitch, *one*.

And I dump it in baggage and get my baggage ticket.

Spend most of the time talking to big corpulent Breton cabdrivers, what I learned in Brittany is 'Dont be afraid to be big, fat, be yourself if you're big and fat.' Those big fat sonumgun Bretons waddle around as tho the last whore of summer war lookin for her first lay. You cant drive a spike with a tack hammer, say the Polocks, well at least said Stanley Twardowicz which is another country I've never seen. You can drive a *nail*, but not a spike.

So I hang around doodling about, for awhile I sigh to eye clover on top of a cliff where I actually could go take a five-hour nap except a lot of little cheap faggots or poets are watching every move I make, it's broad afternoon, how can I go lie down in the tall grass if some Seraglio learns about my remaining $100 on my dear sweet arse?

I'm telling you, I'm getting so suspicious of men, and now less of women, it would make Diana weep, or cough laughing, *one*.

I was really afraid of falling asleep in those weeds, unless nobody saw me sneak into them, to my trapdoor at last, but alas, the Algerians'd found a new home, not to mention Bodhidharma and his boys walking over water from Chaldea (and walking on water wasnt built in a day).

Why perdure the reader's might? The train came at eleven

and I got on the first firstclass coach and got into the first compartment and was alone and put my feet up on the opposite seat as the train rolled out and I heard somebody say to another guy:–

'*Le roi n'est pas amusez.*' (The king is not amused.) ('You frigging A!' I shoulda yelled out the window.)

And a sign said:- 'Dont throw anything out the window' and I yelled '*J'n'ai rien à jeter en dehors du chaussi, ainque ma tête!*' (I got nothing to throw out the window, only my head). My bag was with me – I heard from the other car, '*Ça c'est un Kérouac*,' (Now that's a Kerouac) – I dont even think I was hearing right, but dont be too sure, about not only Brittany but a land of Druids and Witchcraft and Warlocks and Féeries – (not Lebris)—

Let me just brief you on the last happening that I remember in Brest:– afraid to sleep in those weeds, which were not only at edges of cliffs in full sight of people's third storey windows but as I say in full view of wandering punks, I simply in despair sat with the cabdrivers at the cab stand, me on the stone wall – All of a sudden a ferocious vocal fight broke out between a corpulent blue eyed Breton cabdriver and a thin mustachio'd Spanish or I guess Algerian or maybe Provençal cabdriver, to hear them, their 'Come on, if you wanta start something with me *start*' (the Breton) and the younger mustachio 'Rrrratratratra!' (some fight about positions in the cab stand, and there I was a few hours ago couldnt find a cab on Main Street) – I was sitting at this point on the stone curb watching the progress of a lil ole caterpillar in whose fate I was of course particularly fishponded, and I said to the first cab in line at the cab stand:

'In the first place goddamit, *cruise*, cruise thru town for fares, dont hang around this dead railroad station, there might be an Évêque wants a ride after a sudden visit to a donor of the church—'

'Well, it's the union' etc.

I said 'See those two son of a bitches fighting over there, I dont like him.'

No answer.

'I dont like the one who's not the Breton – not the old one, the *young* one.'

The cabdriver looks away at a new development in front of the railroad station, which is, a young vesperish mother toting an infant in her arms and a non-Breton hoodlum on a motorcycle coming to bring a telegram almost knocking her down, but at least scaring the heart out of her.

'That,' I say to my Breton Brother, 'is a *voyou*' (hoodlum) – 'Why did he do it to that lady and her child?'

'To attract all our attention,' he practically leered. He added: 'I have a wife and kids on the hill, across the bay you see there, with the boats . . .'

'Hoodlums are what gave Hitler his start.'

'I'm first in line in this cab stand, let them fight and be hoodlums all they want – When the time comes, the time comes.'

'*Bueno*,' I said like a Spanish pirate of St Malo, '*Garde a campagne*.' (Guard your countryside).

He didnt even have to answer, that big corpulent 220-pound Breton, first in line on the cab stand, his eyes himself would sclowber scubaduba or anything else they wanta throw at 'im, and O most bullshit Jack, the people are not asleep.

And when I say 'the people' I dont mean that created-in-the-textbook mass first called at me at Columbia College as 'Proletariat', and not now called at me as 'Unemployed Disenchanted Ghetto-Dwelling Misfits', or in England as 'Mods and Rods', I say, the People are first, second, third, fourth, fifth, sixth, seventh, eighth, ninth, tenth, eleventh and twelfth in the cabstand line and if you try to bug them, you may find yourself with a blade of grass in your bladder, which cuts finest.

The conductor sees me with my feet on the other seat and yells '*Les pieds a terre!*' (Feet on the ground!) My dreams of being an actual descendant of the Princes of Brittany are shattered also by the old French hoghead blowing at the crossing whatever they blow at French crossings, and of course shattered also by that conductor's enjoinder, but then I look up at the plaque over the seat where my feet had been:–

'*This seat reserved for those wounded in the service of France.*'

So I ups and goes to the compartment next, and the conductor looks in to collect my ticket and I say 'I didnt see that sign.'

He says 'That's awright, but take your shoes off.'

This King will ride second fiddle to anyone so long's he can blow like my Lord.

And all night along, alone in an old passenger coach, Oh Anna Kerenina, O Myshkin, O Rogozhin, I ride back St Brieuc, Rennes, got my brandy, and there's Chartres at dawn—

Arriving in Paris in the morning.

By this time, from the cold of Bretagne, I got big flannel shirt on now, with scarf inside collar, no shave, pack silly hat away into suitcase, close it again with teeth and now, with my Air France return trip ticket to Tampa Florida I'se ready as the fattest ribs in old Winn Dixie, dearest God.

In the middle of the night, by the way, as I marveled at the s's of darkness and light, a mad eager man of 28 got on the train with an 11-year-old girl and escorted her gainingly to the compartment of the wounded, where I could hear him yelling for hours till she gave him the fish eye and fell asleep on her own seat alone – *La Muse de la Départment* and *Le Provinçial à Paris* missed by a coupla years, O Balzac, O in fact Nabokov . . . (The Poetess of the Provinces and the Hick in Paris.) (Whattayou expect with the Prince of Brittany a compartment away?)

So here we are in Paris. All's over. From now on I'm finished with any and all forms of Paris life. Carrying my suitcase I'm accosted at the gates by a cab-hawk. 'I wanta go to Orly' I say.

'Come on!'

'But first I need a beer and a cognac across the street!'

'Sorry no time!' and he turns to other customers calling and I realize I might as well get on my horse if I'm gonna be home tonight Sunday night in Florida so I say:–

'Okay. *Bon, allons.*'

He grabs my bag and lugs it to the waiting cab on the misting sidewalk. A thin-mustached Parisian cabdriver is packing in two ladies with a babe in arms in the back of his hack and meanwhile socking in their luggage in the compartment out back. My fella socks my bag in, asks for 3 or 5 francs, I fergit. I look at the cabdriver as if to say 'In front?' and he says with head 'Yeah.'

I say to myself 'Another thin nosed sonumbitch in *Paris-est-Pourri* shit, he wouldnt care if you roasted your grandmother over coals long as he could get her earrings and maybe gold teeth.'

In the front seat of the little sports taxi I search vainly for an ashtray at my righthand front door. He whips out a weird ashtray arrangement beneath the dashboard, with a smile. He then turns to the ladies in back as he zips through that six-intersection place right outside Toulouse-Lautrec's loose too-much and pipes:–

'Darling little child! How old is she?'

'Oh, seven months.'

'How many others you have?'

'Two.'

'And that's your, eh, Mother?'

'No my aunt.'

'I thought so, of course, she doesn't look like you, of course with my uncanny whatnots – In any case a delightful child, a mother we need speak no further, *of*, and an aunt make all Auvergne rejoice!'

'How did you know we were Auvergnois?!'

'Instinct, instinct, since I am! How are you there, feller, where going?'

'Me?' I say with dismal Breton breath. 'To Florida' (*à Floride*).

'Ah it must be beautiful there! And you, my dear aunt, how many children did you have?'

'Oh – seven.'

'Tsk, tsk, almost too much. And is the little one giving you any trouble?'

'No – not a mite.'

'Well there you have it. All's well, really,' swinging in a wide 70-m.p.h.-arc around the Sainte Chapelle where as I said before the piece of the True Cross is kept and was put there by St Louis of France, King Louis 9th, and I said:–

'Is *that* la Sainte Chapelle? I meant to see it.'

'Ladies,' he says to the back seat, 'you're going where? Oh yes, Gare St-Lazare, yes, here we are – Just another minute' – Zip—

'There we are' and he leaps out as I sit there dumbfounded and blagdenfasted and hauls out their suitcases, whistles for a boy, has them whisked off baby and all, and leaps back into the cab alone with me saying: 'Orly was it?'

'Aye, *mais*, but, Monsieur, a glassa beer for the road.'

'Bah – it'll take me ten minutes.'

'Ten minutes is too long.'

He looks at me seriously.

'Well, I can stop off at a cafe on the way where I can double park and you throw it down real fast 'cause I'm working this Sunday morning, ah, Life.'

'You have one with me.'

Zip.

'Here it is. Out.'

We jump out, run into this cafe thru the now-rain, and duck up to the bar and order two beers. I tell him:–

'If you're in a real hurry I'll show you how to chukalug a beer down!'

'No necessity,' he says sadly, 'we have a minute.'

He suddenly reminds me of Fournier the bookie in Brest.

He tells me his name, of Auvergne, I mine, of Brittany.

At the spot instant when I know he's ready to fly I open my gullet and let a halfbottle of beer fall down a hole, a trick I learned in Phi Gamma Delta fraternity now I see for no small reason (holding up kegs at dawn, and with no pledge cap because I refused it and besides I was on the football team), and in the cab we jump like bankrobbers and ZAM! we're going 90 in the rain slick highway to Orly, he tells me how many kilometers fast he's going, I look out the window and figure it's our cruising speed to the next bar in Texas.

We discuss politics, assassinations, marriages, celebrities, and when we get to Orly he hauls my bag out the back and I pay him and he jumps right back in and says (in French): 'Not to repeat myself, me man, but today Sunday I'm working to support my wife and kids– And I heard what you told me about families in Quebec that had kids by the twenties and twenty-fives, that's too much, that is – Me I've only got two – But, work, yes, yowsah, this and that, or as you say Monsieur thissa and thatta, in any case, thanks, be of good heart, I'm going.'

'Adieu, Monsieur Raymond Baillet,' I say.

The Satori taxidriver of page one.

When God says 'I Am Lived', we'll have forgotten what all the parting was about.

THE WORLD'S GREATEST NOVELISTS NOW AVAILABLE IN TRIAD/GRANADA PAPERBACKS

Ernest Hemingway

The Old Man and The Sea	95p	☐
Fiesta	£1.50	☐
For Whom the Bell Tolls	£1.95	☐
A Farewell to Arms	£1.50	☐
The Snows of Kilimanjaro	£1.50	☐
The Essential Hemingway	£2.25	☐
To Have and Have Not	£1.50	☐
Death in the Afternoon (non-fiction)	£1.95	☐
Green Hills of Africa	95p	☐
Men Without Women	£1.25	☐
A Moveable Feast	£1.50	☐
The Torrents of Spring	95p	☐
Across the River and Into the Trees	£1.95	☐
Winner Take Nothing	£1.50	☐
The Fifth Column	95p	☐

Richard Hughes

A High Wind in Jamaica	£1.25	☐
In Hazard	60p	☐
Fox in the Attic	£1.50	☐
The Wooden Shepherdess	£1.50	☐

James Joyce

Dubliners	£1.50	☐
A Portrait of the Artist as a Young Man	£1.50	☐
Stephen Hero	£1.50	☐
The Essential James Joyce	£2.50	☐
Exiles (play)	£1.25	☐

TF281

THE WORLD'S GREATEST NOVELISTS NOW AVAILABLE IN GRANADA PAPERBACKS

John O'Hara

Ourselves to Know	£1.50	☐
Ten North Frederick	£1.50	☐
A Rage to Live	£1.50	☐
From the Terrace	£2.50	☐
Butterfield 8	95p	☐
Appointment in Samarra	95p	☐

Norman Mailer

The Fight (non-fiction)	£1.25	☐
Cannibals and Christians (non-fiction)	£1.50	☐
The Presidential Papers	£1.50	☐
Barbary Shore	40p	☐
Advertisements for Myself	95p	☐
An American Dream	£1.95	☐
The Naked and The Dead	£2.50	☐
The Deer Park	£1.75	☐

Kingsley Amis

Ending Up	£1.25	☐
I Like It Here	50p	☐
That Uncertain Feeling	50p	☐
Girl 20	40p	☐
I Want It Now	60p	☐
The Green Man	95p	☐

GF881

THE WORLD'S GREATEST NOVELISTS NOW AVAILABLE IN GRANADA PAPERBACKS

Jack Kerouac

Big Sur	£1.50	☐
Visions of Cody	£2.25	☐
Doctor Sax	£1.25	☐
Lonesome Traveller	£1.50	☐
Desolation Angels	£1.35	☐
The Dharma Bums	£1.50	☐
The Subterranians and Pic	£1.50	☐

John Hersey

The Wall	£1.95	☐
The Child Buyer	95p	☐
The Walnut Door	95p	☐
The War Lover	£1.25	☐
A Single Pebble	95p	☐

All these books are available at your local bookshop or newsagent, or can be ordered direct from the publisher. Just tick the titles you want and fill in the form below.

Name _____

Address _____

_____

Write to Granada Cash Sales
PO Box 11, Falmouth, Cornwall TR10 9EN.

Please enclose remittance to the value of the cover price plus:

UK 45p for the first book, 20p for the second book plus 14p per copy for each additional book ordered to a maximum charge of £1.63.

BFPO and Eire 45p for the first book, 20p for the second book plus 14p per copy for the next 7 books, thereafter 8p per book.

Overseas 75p for the first book and 21p for each additional book.

Granada Publishing reserve the right to show new retail prices on covers, which may differ from those previously advertised in the text or elsewhere.

GF281